THE ILLUSION OF A GIRL

~ A YA Novel Based on a True Story ~

LEEANN WERNER

ISBN: 978-1-7330062-5-5 (paperback)
      978-1-7330062-7-9 (ebook)

Cover and interior design by Tara Mayberry, TeaBerry Creative

This book is dedicated to the Seekers.

Luke 11:9-10

"So, I say to you: Ask and it will be given to you; seek and you will find; knock and the door will be opened to you. For everyone who asks receives; the one who seeks finds; and to the one who knocks, the door will be opened."

ACKNOWLEDGMENTS

Thank you to my family and friends who put up with me and read many drafts of this book. A big thank you to my fellow authors, JJ Crane, Lyn Miller-Lachmann, and Kelley Griffin who generously took the time and provided me with valuable insight.

CHAPTER 1

JESSIE

My heavy social studies book slid from my lap and thudded to the floor as mom's pleading voice needled its way through my bedroom walls.

"You're overreacting, he wasn't eyeing me," Mom said.

I swung my bare feet down and dug my toes into the shabby blue carpet. Grabbing the black elastic band from my wrist, I pulled my hair into a low ponytail and took a deep breath.

"You were flirting with him. I watched you," Dad said.

Perched on the side of my bed, I listened as my parent's loud exchange progressed down the hall, past my bedroom and into theirs. I reached down and shoved my feet into nearby running shoes. I always knew when I needed to run.

"That's ridicu—" Mom's angry voice cut off mid-word. Silence. All the blood rushed to my head as I flew across the hall and skidded to a stop at their door. My hand hovered in the air just an inch from the doorknob.

The bed springs creaked, and Mom gasped as I pushed the door open. Dad had pinned Mom to the foot of the bed and was choking her. Her eyes bugged out of her head, and her pantyhose clad legs kicked uselessly against him. I bounced on the balls of my feet and flapped my hands like a panicked bird. Don't scream, don't scream. I edged my way to the side of the room and used my foot to push off from the wall. I charged toward him with my hands outstretched and shoved him with all the strength I had. The smell of whiskey and bitter body odor stung my nose as I pushed against his damp t-shirt. He toppled off the side of the bed, while my momentum slammed me into their dresser. Pain shot through my shoulder. Grunting, I pushed off the dresser and scrambled to the bathroom in the hall.

The main bathroom was the only place in the house where I could lock him out. His anger would turn toward me now. I don't know why that seemed better. I had to help her.

My thumb kept the lock on the bathroom door pushed in, as my hand gripped the handle. Dad reached the flimsy, fake wood door and pounded his fists against it.

"I'm gettin' in!" he screamed.

His body crashed against the door. The sound and vibration rattled through me. I knew he would get a wire hanger and try to pop out the button that locked the door. The lock offered little protection against the looming, drunk maniac hell bent on getting to me. I didn't want to imagine what he would do.

Sweat beaded on my forehead. I swatted my hair to the side and pressed my shoulder against the door, digging my tennis shoes into the pink carpeting. I desperately wished Brian was home to help me. Dad's fist slammed into the door again.

"Stop it! Stop now," Mom said.

"Get out of my way," he said. Dad's retreating voice told me he was headed to their bedroom. He was going for the wire hanger.

This was it. Swallowing hard, I turned the knob. The door opened soundlessly, and I sprinted toward the sliding glass door in the family room. My tennis shoes silent against the carpet. As I rounded the corner to the family room, he screamed my name from the hallway.

A second later, I grabbed the door handle, slid it open and disappeared into the darkness.

By the time he made it to the sliding glass door, I was crouched behind the bushes in the Gallagher's back yard. The smell of mulch filled my nose as I got up on the balls of my feet with one hand pressed into the dirt to steady myself. If he did come looking, I would have time to run further away. With no street lamps, only a few dim porch lights broke up the darkness.

Dad stepped onto the back porch. "Get back here!" he yelled.

Mom slapped his shoulder. "The whole neighborhood can hear you. Come in the house."

I cringed. The odds he would hit her back were very good, and that would mean I'd have to run back to the house to defend her, again, which is how this whole night started. He jerked away from her and stumbled back into the house.

I eased out of my crouched position and blood flow tingled back into my feet. I moved to the back wall of the Gallaghers' house, and hid behind their hydrangea shrubs. I wasn't sure if Dad would get industrious and find a flashlight to come and look for me.

Now I would wait until he passed out. I dimmed the light on my phone, and hoped Brian wouldn't come home anytime soon. At least my brother had been spared tonight's adventure.

The warm air made my wait comfortable. I stared straight ahead into the darkness, listening to my heart rate slow, my mind blank. I wriggled my butt searching for a softer place and rested my head against the brick wall. The TV, and the voices of our neighbors, Ted and Alyssa, broke into my thoughts. The peaceful monotony of their conversation was oddly comforting.

Sometime later, my phone dinged: *Come back, he's asleep.*

I didn't acknowledge the message, but headed toward our house. I crept up to their bedroom window, placed my hands lightly against the brick and listened.

The familiar sound of my dad's loud snoring greeted me. My muscles relaxed a bit. Mom stood by the sliding glass door waiting for me.

"I'm sorry. You okay?" she said. I glared at her stress-lined face and pressed-together lips. She clasped and unclasped her hands in perpetual motion.

"Whatever. Nothing changes, so don't talk to me," I replied.

She hovered behind me as I huffed back to my room to grab a blanket and pillow off my bed. The temporary bed on the bathroom floor wasn't comfy, but at least I would have some barrier between me and my father. I never knew when the other shoe, full of horrible, slimy, dead things, would drop.

CHAPTER 2

JESSIE

I folded the initial chapters of the paperback book under my current page and immersed myself in Pecola's black and white world once again.

"What're you reading?" Rebecca used her finger to push the book cover into view.

"*The Bluest Eye*," it's on the school's banned book list. I'm reading them all one by one," I said.

"Any good?" Rebecca asked.

"It's brutal, but interesting," I said.

What I didn't say was that I could relate to the dark, hateful humans portrayed in the book. I leaned against the wall and waited for the first bell to ring. Our high school, Valley Christian, was a long, two-story, cinder-block rectangle surrounded by mature trees and dense woods. The pervasive greenery seeped in through the mostly glass entrance, tinging the school lobby an eerie gray-green. The white halls and florescent lighting made it feel a little institutional, but I didn't mind. I was safe here.

I winced and adjusted my shoulder against the white-washed wall. The memory of my crash into my parent's dresser flashed through my mind. The cold penetrated the painful bruise and brought some relief. Rebecca didn't notice as she dug in her backpack.

My eyes locked with the large blue eyes of a boy across the hall. He was very cute—thick black brows, black hair. Tall too, around six feet.

I glanced away. For the past two weeks, we'd been playing this staring game. It gave me an odd sense of control.

"Don't look now, but see the guy across the hall?" I asked.

Rebecca, my bestie and neighbor since kindergarten, shifted her position and pretended to stretch. "Which one?"

"Black hair."

"Ah, okay," Rebecca said.

"He stares at me every morning." I kept my eyes glued to her and pretended to be unaware of him.

"He's cute," she said

"Yeah, he is. Maybe he'll actually speak to me at some point."

"You're too scary." She elbowed me and we both laughed.

The bell rang, and we joined the mass of kids streaming up the stairwell to the second floor. I made it to my locker, spun the lock's dial and opened it. I pulled out what I needed from my backpack.

Ally and Kristi, my blond counterparts in shenanigans, stood at their lockers as well. The beauty of lockers being assigned by grade and last name in alphabetical order ensured we were always together.

"What's up?" I said as we walked toward homeroom together.

"A whole lot of nothing, as usual. I'm so tired, seriously, I could lie down in this hallway and go to sleep," Kristi said.

"What time did you go to bed?" I asked.

"Around midnight or so."

"You know, simple math tells you if you go to bed at midnight and get up at six in the morning, you're not getting enough sleep."

"Whatever, don't talk to me about math." She kicked her leg up from behind and hit my butt with her foot. Good thing my ass wasn't bruised.

"So polite." I gave her a mock smile and slid into my desk sideways to continue our conversation. Holly, who sat across from me, joined in as well. I propped my feet on Kristi's chair and leaned toward them.

"I've followed him on Twitter and Instagram. I messaged him a few times, but no response," Holly frowned.

"Who?" I asked.

"Alex Corbin."

I had heard the name but wasn't sure who it was. "Oh, you'll have to point him out to me."

"Will do." She winked at me. "He's hot."

I loved her flirty attitude. We shared the same first period, so when the bell rang, we walked to our first class together.

As we rounded the corner, her eyes darted to the side and she whispered, "That's him."

I followed her glance to the boy with the big blue eyes. My mouth became sawdust dry. He stood outside his classroom, joking with his friends. I hadn't noticed before, but apparently, he had class right next to me.

"Oh, okay." I scratched my neck. Here come the hives.

We lingered in the doorway. "You've got to give him my number and ask him for his," Holly said.

She leaned into me and insistently pressed the note with her number into my palm. I had to give her a little credit; she wasn't afraid to go for what she wanted—via a COURIER.

"What? You want me to just go up to him and ask for his number?" *She's lost her mind.*

"Yes," she said bluntly, and pushed me toward Alex and his group of friends. "Hurry up before the bell rings."

Her earnest face demanded action. No use arguing, she was going to get her way no matter what. I shrugged.

Fine. I peeled my tongue off the roof of my mouth.

Alex moved toward me as soon as he noticed my approach.

"Hey, uh...my friend Holly wants me to give you her number, and she hoped to get yours," I stammered.

Holy crap. We're five years old.

I kept looking from the floor to his face and then back again. The black and white tile floor was suddenly interesting.

"Who wants my number?" He reached out his hand to take the note from me.

I turned to indicate Holly, standing in the doorway of our classroom, with her pretty face and long wavy red hair. She smiled tentatively at us.

"Okay. Thanks," he said.

Although my eyes were on the floor, I could feel his stare burn into my brain.

"But I want your number," he said.

My head snapped up. His eyes sparkled under his thick, black brows, and his black hair curled slightly around his face. My cheeks flushed with heat.

Asking for my number was not how this was supposed to go. Holly would kill me.

"Uh...okay," I said. Speech had deserted my brain. I backed away toward my class. The second bell sounded. I chanced a look back; he hadn't moved. He stood there, still looking at me.

Holly wanted all the non-existent details from our short exchange. I didn't know how to tell her he had asked for my number. I sighed with exasperation and said for the fifth time, "Yes, he took your number, yes, he said he would give you his later and no, he didn't say when. Next time, you go talk to him."

Guilt made me grumpy.

The moment Alex asked for my phone number played over and over in my mind for the rest of the day. I remembered his twinkling blue eyes and intense stare.

The next morning, I got up early to straighten my frizz-prone hair. A genetic gift my mother had passed onto me. After I ran the straightener over it for the thousandth time, I decided it looked good enough. It would only take a hint of moisture though and *bam*, it would be a fuzzy mess. I sprayed an excessive amount of hairspray and peered at myself through the fog. I glanced at my phone. Time to leave, if I wanted to catch my bus. I unplugged the straightener, stopped to get my backpack and headed into the gray, gloomy morning. I crossed my arms tightly over my chest. My long-sleeved cotton t-shirt wasn't a good choice. Ohio mornings could be chilly, but nice and sunny by the afternoon. The bus pulled up and I gratefully stepped into its warmth. I plopped down next to Rebecca.

"You excited?" Rebecca asked, practically bouncing in her seat.

"About what?" I said. She just stared at me. I knew exactly what she was asking.

As soon as we walked in, I noticed Alex with his group of friends, checking out everyone who entered the school. Was he looking for me? As soon as Rebecca and I made it to our spot, he appeared next to me with a big smile.

"Hey, how's it going?" He gazed down at me, sliding a hand into his pocket.

He wore a button-down, pale blue shirt and dark jeans. I breathed in his clean soap smell. His hair was still damp from his morning shower. I was so jealous of easy hair care.

He stood close to me as we talked. His warm arm touched my arm. I wanted to lean into his warmth.

"What classes do you have first period?" His eyes moved from me to Rebecca.

"English," I said.

"Social Studies," said Rebecca.

"I have Geometry. It sucks." He shrugged his shoulders, and grinned. The look floored me. He was hot.

He continued chatting with us as the bell rang. I liked that he included Rebecca in our conversation.

He followed me to my locker and leaned against the one next to mine, his body turned toward me. Our body heat created a warm inclusive bubble.

"Can I get your number?" His blue eyes stared into mine.

"Sure," I said. Telling him no didn't seem like something I was willing to do.

My senses were overloaded with his big, warm, gorgeous presence so close to me. Ally and Kristi stood at their lockers in unusual silence. I could practically feel their ears straining to capture every word. He pulled his phone out of his pocket and entered my number into his contact list. He entered my first and last name. I hadn't given him my name. The second bell sounded.

"Gotta go. Talk to you later." He grinned in supreme satisfaction.

Ally and Kristi were on top of me as soon as Alex cleared hearing range.

"What was that?" Kristi vibrated with hyperactivity. "Did he just walk you to your locker?"

"Yes, he did. I'm in shock." I mock fainted and fell against Ally.

"Did you notice the way he looked at you? It's classic; he's smitten," Ally said. She bumped her hip into mine to emphasize her assessment. My heart raced. As we hurried into homeroom, Kristi excitedly pumped me for details.

"What're you guys freaking out about?" Holly asked as we took our seats.

I frowned and tried to think of something to say, but I tended to blurt information when stressed. "Alex asked for my number."

Cringing, I briefly met her eyes. I could see the sadness I caused. Ally and Kristi slowly turned to face forward in their seats; they wanted no part of this chat.

"I'm sorry, Holly." My face crumpled with the knowledge I had hurt her. "I didn't ask for his number or anything. He just came up to me and started talking."

She stared down at her desk, so I turned forward in my seat. We sat quietly for the rest of homeroom. When the bell sounded for first period, I made sure I stayed with Holly. Before we got to our class, I reached out my hand to her.

"Are we okay? Say the word and I won't speak to him," I said.

"Nah. He's just one guy. Right?" But I knew she was upset. My stomach rested on my feet.

I squeezed her hand. I sensed Alex watching us, but I didn't want to talk to him in front of her.

As the school day went on, Alex stopped by my locker several times, which surprised me. No beating around the bush from this guy: he made his intentions clear. I basked in his attention, like honey to a bee.

"If one more girl asks me if Alex Corbin is coming to your locker, I'm going to be sick," Kristi said, leaning, as if exhausted, against the locker next to mine.

I pushed my books into my locker.

"What? Who's asking you if Alex is coming to my locker?" I said.

"Um, every girl who knows me even slightly." She shut her locker. "Seriously, you're the talk of ninth grade."

"Great, because that's my goal for this year." I shut my locker, made a big-eyed face at Kristi, and we both started to laugh. A swell of pride bloomed in my chest.

The ninth-grade girls were all abuzz with this current information. It wasn't like they could be mad at me for scoring the cutest guy in tenth grade—which he actually was—because it was so obvious he was pursuing me.

I felt bad about it because of Holly. Did I even like him? Or did I just like the attention?

CHAPTER 3

JESSIE

The cheerleaders jumped up and down, shaking their pom-poms as the football team ran into the stadium. Ally and Kristi had made the JV squad, so Rebecca, Holly and I sat in the front row of the bleachers to support them. It was the first football game of the year and perfect sweater weather. As the sun went down, so did the temperature. Every girl participated in the Friday night fashion show of fall sweaters.

Since I was now a proud freshman, I sat with my friends instead of Mom to watch the game. A whistle shrilled and the game began. Brian played wide receiver and caught the first pass. I jumped up to clap and smiled as Ally cheered enthusiastically for him. Her crush on my brother was epic. My eyes searched the sidelines. I spotted Alex after a minute or so. I peeked at Holly to see if she'd noticed. She hadn't. My eyes gravitated back to him. He looked good is his football pants. He texted me before the game, and said he hoped he could see me later. Cheers broke into my thoughts. We had just scored a touchdown.

Jumping to our feet, we all threw red, black and white confetti in the air. Each pocket of my jacket held several containers. A sea of confetti rained down around us. Rebecca and I smiled as we bent down to shake the confetti out of our hair.

"We might as well not bother. I'm sure they'll get another touchdown," I said.

"Yeah, seriously," she answered.

Several plays later, Alex ran out on the field. He was a wide receiver as well. He wore number 88.

Alex caught the ball and gained ten yards before being tackled. Cheers went up on our side, and several girls a few bleachers behind us yelled for number 88.

I glanced back and noticed a girl with blond hair and the number 88 drawn in black on her cheek. Pretty bold to put a guy's number on your face unless he was your boyfriend, and Alex didn't have a girlfriend as far as I knew. He sure didn't act like it. I looked at her too long because her eyes locked onto mine, and she gave me one of those shitty, lips-pressed-together smiles. Crossing my arms over my chest, I turned back around in my seat. What a bitch. I thought she was a sophomore, but I wasn't positive.

My attention turned back to the game. We were pretty much kicking the other team's butt. Brian caught another pass, but was taken down by some huge dude. I stood up, worried, and stared intently as the guy rolled off him. Rebecca and I clasped hands. Brian's teammates ran over to him to help him up. He steadied himself and staggered off the field. Rebecca and I both exhaled in relief.

The game seemed to wrap up quickly after that. Tim, my brother's best friend, came over to us near the end of the fourth quarter.

"Looks like we have this game in the bag," he said. "You ladies ready to go?"

"Yep. Where're we going?" I asked.

"McDonald's. We always Mickey D after the football game." Tim looked at me like I was dumb.

"Just asking. I'm new to high school, remember?" I widened my eyes as I said it.

"Yes, I know. Hence my babysitting duties per your brother's instructions," Tim said.

I leaned close to him and whispered, "Is this your only move to hang out with Rebecca?"

He frowned, shook his head in a quick "no" gesture. My cue to shut up. Tim stared at Rebecca a lot, taking us to McDonald's after the game didn't represent a big hardship.

"Let's leave now so we can actually order food and sit down before it gets nuts in there," he said.

"Okay, wait a sec though, who's the girl a couple of bleachers behind us with 88 drawn on her face?"

He stole a look over his shoulder. "Amanda something. She's a sophomore. Why?"

"She gave me a dirty look for some reason."

"Don't worry about it. You could take her." He pushed my shoulder.

"Yeah, right. I don't think a fight will be necessary," I said.

"Why? I would *loovve* a good girl fight." He laughed.

I rolled my eyes at him in reply.

"Come on, let's go." He motioned for us to get up.

I shot a quick look behind me and Amanda directed another nasty look my way. Frowning, I followed Tim to the car.

Me, Rebecca and Holly packed into McDonald's with what appeared to be the rest of the high school. Ally and Kristi would show up after the game.

"This is so much fun," Rebecca said, smashed next to me in a booth.

"I know." I grinned back at her. It was fun just to watch who was talking to who, how the boys tended to push and mock punch each other and the different girl groups.

"The football players are here." Holly said from across the table. She faced the doors.

A jolt of excitement zipped through me.

I didn't want to act excited in front of Holly, but I didn't know how this would go down or if anything at all would happen. The whole situation sucked. I didn't want to like a guy my friend liked.

Before I could think about it more, Alex appeared beside our table with damp hair from the shower and a bag for takeout. Topher, another sophomore, stood beside him.

"Hey, how's it going?" He directed the question to me but smiled and made eye contact with everyone at the table.

"Good. Great game, I saw your catch." A big smile covered my face. I probably looked like an idiot.

"Thanks." He dug a hamburger out of the bag and then looked around for a place to sit.

I jumped up and offered my seat.

"I don't want to take your seat. Do you want to sit with me over here?" He motioned to a newly vacated table.

"Sure." As I stood up, Topher took my place.

"Would you like something to eat? I don't want to eat in front of you," Alex said.

"I'm good, thanks. I ate already," I said.

"Okay." With one bite, he devoured about half his burger. He swallowed. "Sorry, I'm starving. I didn't get to eat before the game."

"No problem. I eat with Brian most nights, so it would be hard to offend me." I smiled at him, and he responded with the cutest closed-lip smile.

His blue eyes studied me. He shook his fry container at me, indicating I eat some, so I took a few.

"Right, I forgot you're Brian's sister."

"At least you're willing to share food. With Brian I have to guard my plate like I'm in prison." I munched a fry and watched him.

He laughed, and I tried to keep the conversation moving by saying "Brian said you guys have a great team this year." I hoped he couldn't tell that I had no idea what to say.

"Yeah, we do have a lot of good players. I wish I got to play more," he answered between bites.

"It's just the first game. I'm sure they'll put you in more," I said.

As the words left my mouth, the girl from the game, Amanda, showed up beside our table. She put her tray down on the table next to ours.

"Great catch, Alex." She beamed at him and bent down to give him a hug.

"Thanks." He awkwardly hugged her back. I didn't know what to say with her and her buddy sitting so close to us. They would hear everything we said. I picked at my nails in my lap.

Brian approached our table with a frown. Rebecca and Holly followed him with pained expressions.

"Hey, we've got to go. Tracey isn't feeling well," Brian said. He gave Alex a full once over. "What's up?"

"Nothing much," Alex replied.

Brian's frowned deepened. "Come on." He motioned his hand for me to follow.

I stood. "Guess I have to go. I'll talk to you later?"

Alex gently reached out and tugged on the bottom of my sweater. "Wait a sec, we'll go too." Alex signaled Topher, who was talking to Ally. We all made our way out to the parking lot. I noticed Alex didn't say goodbye to Amanda. Thank God.

Since Ally lived near Topher, she rode with them. I wished I could've gone with them. They waved to us before they got into the car. Rebecca, Holly and I scrunched into the backseat of Brian's car. Tracey sat up front.

I leaned forward and put my arms around her shoulders. "Hey, how's it going?"

"Okay, I'm not feeling so hot." She was unusually soft spoken. She patted my arm affectionately.

"I'm sorry," I said.

"It's no biggie. I'm sure I'll be fine by tomorrow." Brian shot Tracey a look of concern and squeezed her hand.

I patted her shoulder, then sat back in my seat.

"Alex really likes you." Holly said close to my ear. The loud radio drowned out our conversation to anyone else.

I didn't know what to say.

"You like him too." She lifted one corner of her mouth in a smile. "I guess I'll let you have him, but just this once," she said and elbowed me.

"Thanks, that's big of you." Relief washed through me. At least we were joking about it.

"What's up with Amanda coming over and sitting next to you guys? Hello, she seems desperate, which is not a good look."

"Yeah, pretty psycho of her," I said.

"Everyone can see Alex is into you, big time."

I glanced down at my lap, but I couldn't stop the huge smile that spread across my face.

The rest of the weekend was a flurry of texting with Alex, a huge goofy grin plastered to my face. I took a deep breath. All this attention felt like oxygen to me.

Monday morning dawned bright and early as it always does for high school students. Even though Alex wouldn't be anywhere near my legs, I carefully shaved them in the shower and let the conditioner soak into my hair a few more minutes. Squeaky clean, I toweled off and got ready quickly.

Unconcerned with my impatience, the bus lumbered to a slow stop in front of our high school. I couldn't wait to get off and see Alex. Would we click in person like we had with texting? I hustled around the corner to our morning spot and there he was. Our eyes met and grins spread across both of our faces. Thinking of nothing else, I walked straight to him, like I had been pulled. Everything around me disappeared. There was only Alex.

"Hey, it's good to see you." His sparkling blue eyes searched mine.

"It's good to see you." I stood just a few inches away from him. He reached out his hand and pulled me close with his warm arm circled around my waist. Goosebumps rose on my neck and spread down my back. My shoulder fit under his, and our hips were perfectly aligned.

It felt so good to be next to him. I couldn't remember ever feeling quite this giddy. I became aware of other people again and noticed Rebecca had followed me into the group. Ally was there too, talking to Topher. I couldn't tell you what we talked about. I was too busy soaking up the physical thrill of being pressed close to him. He smelled freshly showered to.

The bell rang and we headed up the stairs. He leaned against the locker next to mine, one finger hooked into the loop in my jeans as I opened the door to get my books.

"I was thinking when we could get together, you know, outside of school," he said.

"Yeah? Like what?"

"Do you want to ride home with me after the football game on Friday?" he asked.

"I'd like to, but I don't think my parents will let me. Maybe we could meet at the movies on Saturday?"

"Yeah, we'll figure something out," he said. He gently tugged at my belt loop "See you later.

I hated my parents immensely at that moment for being ridiculously strict.

Ally and Kristi waited until Alex walked away before they joined me.

"That seems to be going well," Ally said as she waggled her brows at me.

"You know that face you make is ridiculous, right?" I laughed.

"Don't try to distract me from my fact-finding mission. I want all the sloppy details," she said.

"No sloppy details as of yet, but hey, maybe you can help in that department?"

"What?" Ally said.

"Help me figure out how to meet up with Alex somewhere without my parents knowing."

"Hmm, I love that. I'll put my secret hookup skills to use," Ally gleefully rubbed her palms together.

Smiling I said, "You do that."

CHAPTER 4

BRIAN

Footsteps pounded down the hallway. My bedroom door slammed open and Dad barreled into my room.

"Get up!" he screamed.

He grabbed my upper arm and jerked me from bed. I pushed my morning wood down in my shorts.

"What?" I said, trying to pull my arm free.

"Dumb ass. I'll kill you for this." He kept my arm in a vice grip as he pulled me down the hall.

I caught a whiff of his breath, it was flammable. Shit. My chest tightened.

My mind raced, what had I done to piss him off. Realization dawned a moment later and fear crawled up my spine. Why did I think Mom would help me with anything? Why did I even tell her?

We came to a halt at the dining room table. Mom's red rimmed eyes looked up at me with remorse.

"You need to tell me what you told your mother," Dad demanded. He squeezed my arm painfully.

I hated being scared of him. He took a menacing step toward me. I flinched backward out of his reach.

"Tracey's pregnant," I said. Tears stung my eyes.

"*You* will let her know you want nothing to do with it," Dad said, as he jabbed his finger at me.

Baby, our dog, with her big brown eyes cowered under the dining room table. I lifted my eyes to his. "I'm not going to say that," I said.

"You little punk. You'll do exactly what I tell you to do." His fist smashed into my mouth before I could react.

Jessie appeared in the dining room in her white, knee-length nightgown. Her eyes were wild as she assessed the situation.

"What's wrong?" she screamed. "Leave him alone!" She ran at Dad and pushed him away from me.

I watched in horror as her push made him take a few steps back to regain his balance. His furious gaze shifted to her.

Like a snake strike, Dad's hand smacked the side of her head. Jessie's thin frame staggered under the blow. I would kill him.

"Don't you touch her!" I lunged toward him. I was going to strangle him until he choked.

My six foot two frame rammed into Dad's slightly shorter one. The dishes in the china cabinet rattled. We tumbled backward into the living room.

"STOP! STOP! PLEASE!" Mom's hands were pressed against her head.

I was intent on getting my hands around his neck. Dad pushed me off with his legs. He crawled toward Mom and noticed her face. The mindless rage seemed to drain out of him. Mom's body shook with sobs. Dad reached for her and pulled her into his embrace. I moved toward Jessie. We backed out of the kitchen and into the hallway. We kept our eyes glued to our father, as if we were prey. You never turned your back on a predator.

I propelled Jessie back to my bedroom. My lip was bleeding. She held her hand cupped to her ear.

"You okay?" I stooped down to look at her. "I'm going to kill him."

"Yeah, I'm okay," she said.

My blue eyes met her brown ones. Her eyes were tearing up. I turned her head to the side to assess the damage. Her ear was swollen, but her face wasn't marked.

"What was that about?" she asked. "Why's Dad hitting you?"

Typically, my dad would have some reason why he struck us. Undoubtedly crazy, but there would be a reason. He might hit me for something as little as not cleaning the garage. You could never guess what he would do, but the punishments far exceeded the crimes.

Exhausted, I pulled on a T-shirt, and pushed my hair off my sweaty forehead. I couldn't meet her eyes.

"Just drop it," I said.

"Drop it. Seriously?"

I put up my hand and sat down on the edge of the bed. Choked sobs racked my body. I couldn't hold them back. Jessie scooted next to me, shoulder to shoulder.

"It's okay," She whispered repeatedly.

It took a few minutes, but I got myself together and used the bottom of my shirt to wipe my face. My lip throbbed. I grabbed the ibuprofen off my dresser.

"You want some ibuprofen for your head?" I dry swallowed three of them. I popped ibuprofen all the time.

I shook some out in Jessie's shaking hand.

"I'm going back to bed," I said. I didn't know how else to deal with this.

I flopped back down on my bed. Dad would leave us alone now. He wouldn't want to upset Mom again. I dug around my bed covers for my phone. I found it and checked for any messages from Tracey. There weren't any, and it was too early to contact her. I pushed my pillow more securely under my head. I could hear their murmured conversation in the kitchen and wondered what excuses he was giving her. I couldn't imagine any excuse that would make his actions acceptable.

Jessie left my room and came back a minute later with her comforter and pillow and laid them on the floor. When she had bad dreams as a kid, she would do the same thing.

Dad's heavy footfalls crossed the linoleum kitchen floor. The door to the garage opened and closed. He must have left for his shift at the police station; the house seemed to exhale.

A few moments later, Baby, our half Chihuahua and something mutt, came into my room. Jessie lifted her comforter and pulled Baby to her chest.

A ray of sun found its way into my room. My heavy lids closed as I watched the dust motes float slowly downward.

CHAPTER 5

JESSIE

A few hours later, Mom's hand on my shoulder and her soft voice woke me. "Will you go to the store with me? I would love some company."

"What time is it?" I asked.

"Eleven o'clock."

"I guess," I grumbled. I moved Baby over and wearily got up from the floor. A quick glance at Brian confirmed he was still asleep. I covered Baby back up, and headed to the bathroom.

Standing in the shower for a few minutes, I allowed the spray of water to soak my head and wake me up. I ran the soapy washcloth over my body, shampooed and conditioned my hair and got out.

As steam evaporated from the mirror, a girl with dark hair and a pained expression stared back at me. I didn't recognize myself. My thoughts didn't seem like they belonged to the girl in the mirror. Fear settled in my stomach like a large, cold stone. I knew it was me, but it didn't feel like it. My thoughts existed outside of my physical body. With a trembling hand, I slowly dragged my fingers downward to blur the image. My scalp prickled as I backed away from the mirror and slid down the bathroom wall, still wrapped in my towel.

I desperately wanted this out-of-body feeling to go away. With my fingers pressed to my temples, I shivered and whispered, "3130 Brookhaven Drive. I live at 3130 Brookhaven Drive. My name is Jessie. I am Jessie." I prayed repeating my name and address would put my brain back where it belonged.

"God, please make this feeling go away. Please God, make this feeling go away." I wondered if this was what it felt like to lose your mind. My sanity would be the toll for the constant uncertainty and fear in my home.

"Jessie, how much longer 'til you're ready?" Mom asked outside the bathroom door.

Her voice broke me out of my panicked trance.

"Not long," I answered. Slowly, I rose from the pink carpeted floor and got dressed. I pulled my still-wet hair into a ponytail. I kept my eyes glued to the floor. I was afraid my reflection in the mirror would kick off the disconnected feeling again.

I settled myself into the front seat of the car and buckled up. Mom glanced over at me.

"You okay?" she asked.

"No. Are you?" I glared back at her. Did she seriously think I would be okay? Frowning, I folded my arms across my stomach. Mom just sighed. She didn't try to talk again. She knew I would quickly shut down her weak attempts.

As we drove to the store, I stared out the window at the passing scenery: our neighborhood with large maple trees, soft rolling hills, ranch-style homes and kids' toys in almost every yard. The landscape shifted to flat land and brown corn fields once we drove a few miles out of our subdivision. In the summer, the fields were lush with tall, dark green corn stalks and moist earth, but now, in the fall, only dried, cut-down stalks remained. I rolled down the window and let the breeze soothe my brain.

Finally, retail stores appeared as we entered Stanton's downtown. We arrived at the grocery store and quickly went through each aisle picking up our usual grocery items. I ambled through the aisles, not saying much, and mulled over the events of the morning.

In the cereal aisle, we ran into lavender-haired Mabel, one of the older ladies from church. I guessed she was in her early eighties. In fact, all the ladies near Mabel's age had lavender hair. And why did they jingle with every step? Once you got old, were you assigned a bell to clip on your clothes and lavender hair dye?

"Hi Jan, Jessie, how are you?" Mabel greeted both of us.

I wanted to say, *Hi Mabel, Dad punched Brian this morning and due to our constant abuse, I'm losing my mind. How about you?*

"We're good," Mom said. "How are you?"

Her response prevented mine, which was probably a good thing.

Let's all pretend everything is fine. They continued to chit-chat while I sauntered away under the pretense of cereal selection. To avoid any additional conversation, I stared intently at the various brands of Raisin Bran until Mom and Mabel stopped talking.

We finished shopping and headed to the parking lot. It was a windy fall day and my long ponytail whipped at my face as I loaded the groceries into the trunk. The warm wind washed over my skin like a caress. I loved the fall weather. It wasn't too hot or too cold, but perfectly dry and sunny. As I loaded the last of the groceries into the trunk, the image of Brian's face from this morning flashed in my head. It was the look of despair in his eyes. More than anything, I hated Dad for hurting Brian. I didn't like it when Dad hurt Mom either, but it pissed me off that she kept him around when she could have sent him packing.

During our silent ride back home, I glared out the window and noticed nothing. All the while, my anger built. I hated Dad more for hitting Brian then me. I hated him for hitting me too, but it hurt me more if he hit Brian. As Mom slowly pulled into the garage, I couldn't hold back any longer.

"Are you going to continue to let Dad treat Brian the way he did this morning?" I demanded.

Mom took a deep breath. "I don't want to argue with you about your dad." Her tall frame sagged under the weight of my question. Her blue eyes looked back at me with utter fatigue. Her blue eyes, just like Brian's.

"I don't want to argue with you either, but I do want you to do something about our crappy existence."

"Jessie! Watch your language."

She was silent as we loaded all the groceries into the house. Then she put her small hands flat on the counter and leaned against it. "You don't need to be involved with Brian's issue," she said.

"I'm involved when all the yelling scares me out of bed," I said. "Do you think Dad's way is a good way to solve problems?"

"No, but I will talk to your dad about it. All parents make mistakes. The important thing is that Dad loves you and Brian," Mom said.

I shook my head as if to clear my ears. "I'm sorry…I thought you lived here. Are you out of your mind? He may love you, but he doesn't love Brian and me. I hoped you noticed," I said.

"That's not true. You're being dramatic. I love Dad and I know he loves us," Mom said.

Dumbfounded, I grabbed the jug of detergent, and with all the anger and frustration roaring inside me, hurled it across the kitchen. It smacked against the refrigerator door with a loud thud.

Mom gaped at me.

"You're killing me!" I shouted. "Is there no limit to what you'll allow him to do to us? I'm dying every day in this house. Dad doesn't love us. I've feared him for as long as I can remember. Dad loves alcohol, that's it. Isn't that how alcoholics behave? It's all about them, all the time!"

I gripped the back of the dining room chair for support. An unbearable pain seared through my head. Mom's continued betrayal left a gaping wound in my chest. She came toward me with her arms open. I held up my hand, palm first, to stop her. I wanted her to hurt as much as I hurt.

"Understand me: I don't love him and neither does Brian. He hasn't done anything to deserve our love. Once Brian and I leave this house, we won't be back. You can have Dad and live with him the rest of your life, but don't expect us to be around. No matter how hard you cry, or how many times you call, I won't come back to this house. You'll be stuck with him and that's what you deserve." I spat the words; their bitterness tasted like poison on my lips. My throat was raw and dry with pain. Tears and snot mixed on my chin. I wanted to tear down everything in the house. Rage burned in my chest like a pillar of fire. If it escaped my body, it would burn its way through our atmosphere and crack the earth.

I turned and headed for the front door.

Mom called out to me, "Are you trying to break my heart?"

With my hand on the doorknob, I said, "You've already broken mine."

As I strode through our leaf-filled front yard, I heard the front door squeak open and shut again. Brian joined me a minute later.

We walked down our winding street side by side. Big silver maple trees bordered each side of our street.

"Why did you start with Mom?" he asked. "That was pretty intense."

"Because I can't take it anymore, I can't stand to see him hurt you and I'm tired of living like this. He's never going to stop drinking and his temper is getting worse."

Tears rolled down my face and onto my t-shirt. I didn't care if the neighbors saw me.

Brian awkwardly patted me on the back. "It's going to be okay. We can get through this."

"Can we?" my voice cracked. I wanted to tell him about my mental breakdown this morning, but couldn't think of how.

He didn't respond, and we continued in silence. He rubbed his right fist in the palm of his left hand repeatedly, something he did when he was excited or nervous.

"Look, a blue jay," he said, pointing to a brilliant bird sitting on one of the lower branches of a tree. The jay noisily called for his mate while displaying his beautiful feathers. Brian was trying to distract me. He knew I loved birds. I envied their ability to fly away.

A few minutes later, he said, "I can't believe you threw the jug of detergent. I hope we can get the dent out of the fridge." He winked at me and chuckled. "I listened from the hallway."

"Yeah, I figured," I said.

"Come on, get your shit together," he said, shaking my shoulder.

I wiped my face with my hand, and lifted one corner of my mouth. I seriously doubted things would be okay.

I still didn't know why Dad had punched him, but I suspected it had something to do with Tracey. I watched as Brian rubbed his fist in the palm of his left hand repeatedly.

CHAPTER 6

BRIAN

I quickly adjusted my junk as we walked silently together. How messed up could our lives get? I asked Mom for help and what does she do? She tells Dad, which led to an arm-jerking, mouth-punching wake-up call.

I don't know why I had even thought she would help me. She always let Dad run the show. They were both assholes. I couldn't remember any good times with him. In fact, my memories of him were crazy. Standing in our driveway, in the dead of winter, Mom dressed in her robe, with me scared out of my mind behind her. I was just tall enough to reach her chest. Jessie stood behind me, both of us in our pajamas. Jessie's hand clenched mine as Mom screamed for Dad to come into the house. He had laid down on his back in the middle of the driveway. At the time, I thought his bald head must be cold on the concrete. He was so shit-faced, he probably didn't feel the cold. Even then, I hoped a car would run over him, and pop his head like a melon.

The image jolted me back to our present walk. I glanced over at my sister and dug my hands deeper in my pockets. What a nightmare weekend this had been.

"Come on, let's go back home. I'm starving," I said.

We turned back toward the house. I had no idea what I was going to do.

. . .

Fortunately, Monday's wake-up call was the annoying digital beeping of my iPhone. Much better than the punch yesterday. I shuffled to the bathroom, took a leak and peered into my bloodshot eyes. My grainy eyes were a testament to my lack of sleep. But nothing was going to prevent me from hustling over to Tracey's house first thing this morning. As I pulled into her driveway, she opened the front door. My beautiful girl with her with her big green eyes.

I got out of the car and opened her car door for her. *My dad is a militant asshole, so yeah, I have excellent manners.* Before she got in the car, I gave her a quick kiss.

"How're you doing, babe?"

She looked up at me with tear-filled eyes.

"I'm bleeding." Her bottom lip trembled. "I don't know what to think."

My whole body tensed in panic. "Should I take you to the hospital?"

"We'll have to go to Planned Parenthood after school. They won't call my parents."

"Will you be okay until then?" I was desperate to make her better. Her face was pale. "How much are you bleeding?"

"It's like my period," she said.

"Are you sure we shouldn't go to the doctor now?" I could literally feel my balls creeping back into my body in panic.

"If we skip school, they'll call my mom. And we can't go to the regular doctor, they'll notify my mom too," she sighed.

I put my arm around her and pulled her close to me. "What does it mean if you're bleeding?" It killed me that I did this to my girl.

"It could be nothing or I could be losing the baby. Planned Parenthood will have to examine me," she crossed her arms over her stomach.

My mouth went dry, "Oh my God."

I rubbed my hand across my forehead. What else could I do?

She leaned into me and I gave her a long hug. "Let's just go to school. That's all we can do right now," she said softly.

"Yeah, okay." My entire body was drenched with sweat. As I reversed down the driveway my cherry bomb mufflers purred to life.

I protectively put my arm around her waist as we walked through the school parking lot. She appeared to be walking okay, which made me feel a little better. Even with all this shit going on, I loved the feel of her walking beside me, her smell and soft skin.

My best friend Tim came running over as soon as he saw me. I stepped in front of Tracey to absorb the impact. Tim's chest bounced off my upheld hand.

"What's up?" Tim said.

"Watch out! Tracey isn't feeling well," I said.

"Oh, sorry," he said, and glanced at her.

"It's okay, I'm fine," she said.

We walked into school. I nodded at Tim. "I'll catch up with you in minute."

"Sure."

"How did your talk with your mom go?" Tracey asked as we stood at her locker. Her big green eyes studied my face with concern.

"Not well. She won't help us. Her main concern consisted of no one finding out I got you pregnant."

"She's not very worried about how you feel, is she?" Tracey frowned.

"No, Mom is all about what everyone else thinks of our family. It's bullshit." I didn't mention Mom and Dad's fight, Dad's explosion, and especially not him punching me. No need to upset her more. My stomach knotted in panic. I desperately needed to do something.

It was the longest school day of my life, but finally the last bell rang. I wanted to pick Tracey up and run to my car in the school parking lot.

I noticed a few protesters with anti-abortion signs as I neared Planned Parenthood. It was surreal to me that it was located near a grocery store. I shielded Tracey from the protestors' view and guided her into the building.

Once she was taken for her examination, I rushed out of the building. I paced near my car in the parking lot. They wouldn't let me go with her. As the only guy, all eyes rested on me. A cloud of blame seemed to surround me.

My head was hot, like an impending meltdown. Forty-five minutes had ticked by since the nurse had taken her back. Shit, I had to get back to school and get ready for the football game tonight.

I strode back into the clinic and handed the receptionist my driver's license. She sat in what looked to be a bulletproof glass and metal enclosure. The whole setup freaked me out. It made me want to wear my sports cup and protect my boys.

I sat near the door where Tracey would come back out. An older lady sitting about ten feet from me gave me the stink eye every time I looked up. I wanted to tell her to fuck off in the worst way. I ran my hand through my hair for the tenth time and stared unseeingly at my phone. The door opened, and finally Tracey appeared. I rushed over to her.

"You okay? What did they say?" I put my arm around her and pulled her close.

"Let's get out of here first," she said.

I settled Tracey in the car, shut her door and got in on the driver's side. I turned toward her and waited for her to speak.

"They said I miscarried. They don't know why, but usually there is something wrong with the baby if you miscarry in the first trimester." Her bottom lip pushed out and her face scrunched together.

"I'm sorry, honey." I took her in my arms.

"I know now isn't a good time to have a baby, but it still makes me sad. It was our baby." She sobbed into my shoulder. It felt like a knife plunged into my heart. I would do anything to make this right.

"I'm sad too. We'll have a baby someday. I promise you."

"Don't say that. We don't know where our lives will go. You're going to college. I'm going to college."

"I know that we'll be together. No matter what happens, you're it for me. Nothing will change how I feel about you." My eyes searched hers. I knew from the moment we met. It was undeniable, and I didn't care that I was only seventeen.

"I do. It's kind of scary. I didn't want to feel like forever with someone now. I always thought it would come later, but here you are, my handsome guy," she said, trying to smile.

She put her hand on my cheek and kissed me. She wiped the tears from my face. I didn't realize I had been crying. I hugged her close to me and we sat silently for a few minutes.

She nuzzled her head under my chin and said, "Take me home please. I need to lay down."

"Okay." I kept my hand on her thigh as we drove, and she leaned against my arm with her eyes closed. Once we pulled into her driveway, I helped her out of the car and escorted her to the front door.

"I have to get ready for the game tonight, but text me and let me know how you're feeling," I said.

"Okay." She gave me a kiss and said goodbye.

Her mom opened the front door as I turned to walk away. "Hey, Brian."

"Hi, Mrs. Stephens." She looked at me and then at Tracey.

"Is something wrong?" she asked.

Tracey piped up, "Mom, there's nothing wrong. My stomach is upset. That's all." She rolled her eyes in mock annoyance.

Too scared to move, I froze.

"Oh, okay. Forgive me for asking." Mrs. Stephens said it sarcastically, but kept her eyes glued to mine. She knew something was up.

If she figured out what was up and called my parents, my dad would finish killing me. No question.

I swallowed and said, "See you later."

As I walked back to my car, the setting sun bathed the neighborhood in a pinkish-gold light. Well-kept yards, bikes in the driveway and distant shrieks of kids playing. Life could look great on the surface, but it didn't mean monsters weren't lurking below.

CHAPTER 7

JESSIE

My next class wasn't a class. Coach Wilson had nominated me to be an office worker during my study period. He knew me well since he'd coached me in track in seventh and eighth grade. My office worker duties entailed running errands for our school counselor, Mrs. Palmer, and the principal's assistant, Mrs. Wills.

I wanted to talk to Mrs. Palmer about the mirror episode. I didn't know what was wrong with me. Even thinking about it made me feel unsettled. What if I had a brain tumor or something? Thankfully, she was in her office alone.

"Mrs. Palmer, do you have time to talk for a few minutes?" I asked.

"Absolutely! Come in and shut the door behind you."

I went into her office and took a seat. She put down her pen. Her brunette hair brought out her light blue eyes, which laser-focused on mine.

"What can I do for you?" she said.

"I'm not sure how to start. I…I'm worried about something that happened." I took a deep breath and tried to let it out slowly.

"It's okay, try to relax and just tell me what happened," she said.

"It's weird and sounds crazy, but sometimes when I look in the mirror, this feeling comes over me, and I don't recognize the person being reflected. I know it sounds weird and it's hard to explain. I do know who I am, but on the other hand, it seems like I'm outside of myself. It's like my brain doesn't go with my body." I rubbed my forehead.

With furrowed brows, she said, "I'm sorry that you're having that experience."

"Is that a symptom of a brain tumor or something?"

She chuckled. "Let's not jump to conclusions, but if I do think it's something medical, we'll get you to the doctor," she said.

"Okay." I smiled in relief.

"Are you going through something very stressful right now?" she asked.

"No, nothing I can think of right away. Does stress cause this?"

"Stress can cause many physical problems. I could make some assumptions, but I don't want to do that. Give me some more detail so I can understand what's going on when you feel like this," she said.

"Okay," I said tentatively.

"Is school going okay for you?"

"Oh, yeah, I like high school so far."

"Okay, how about at home?"

I hesitated and then blurted, "I don't really like my parents." I wanted to smack my own head. When would I stop blurting information?

"Being a teenager is hard for the teen and the parents," she said, and smiled at me affectionately.

Someone knocked. Mrs. Palmer glanced through the small window in the door and held up one finger.

"I do want to talk again, but tonight I volunteer at the Veterans Association Hospital, so after school wouldn't work." She studied her appointment calendar.

"I have choir practice after school anyway." I stood up and started to leave.

"All right, we can talk tomorrow and set up some time. I'm glad you came in to talk to me," she said.

"Thank you." I nodded. She wasn't fake-nice, like some adults. As soon as I left her office, I sat down in front of the office computer and Googled 'feeling like you're outside of your body.' I clicked on WebDoc's entry. As I read the description, a few things jumped out at me.

"Depersonalization disorder is marked by periods of feeling disconnected or detached from one's body and thoughts (depersonalization)."

That's how it felt.

"Depersonalization also might be a symptom of other disorders, including some forms of substance abuse, post-traumatic stress disorder, certain personality disorders, seizure disorders and certain other brain diseases."

My eye kept going back to personality disorders. I would mention these disorders the next time I talked to Mrs. Palmer. I let out a long sigh; what in the hell was wrong with me? The rest of the school day went quickly after my meeting with words like depersonalization disorder repeating in my head.

. . .

Checking out the bathroom window told me it was nice and sunny outside. I finished brushing my teeth and leaned over the bathroom counter to examine them closely in the mirror. While slowly running a finger over my top teeth, I paused and pushed slightly on the front two. They felt secure. My two front teeth were porcelain veneers since Brian had knocked out my real teeth.

His fault, but I'd started the fight.

Thinking back to when it happened, the summer after fifth grade, I recalled my nickname with a smile: Beaver. It didn't bother me at that age, and one look in the mirror confirmed I did in fact resemble a beaver. Dark hair, big brown eyes, bucked and gapped front teeth.

The day was what I liked to call a 'burner.' Humidity at eighty percent and the temperature over ninety degrees. The only way we could stand the heat involved us in a pool.

We waded through the heavy, moist and unbelievably stifling air to our neighbor's house—Ted and Alyssa—and availed ourselves of their pool. We weren't shy since they'd offered to let us use their pool anytime. We made our way around the house and into the backyard. There sat the above ground pool in all its cool, blue beauty. The surface of the pool shimmered white and blue in invitation. I dropped my towel and ran. I shimmied up the ladder and jumped into the pale cool water. The water rushed over my heated body like a blessing. Brian quickly followed me into the pool and we both floated on our backs, enjoying the relief from the heat. As I pushed my foot against the bottom of the pool, it connected with something hard and bristled. I straightened up and looked down. A brush they used to clean the pool laid on the bottom. Dunking under the water, I picked it up. I toyed with the bristles and then swam over to the side of the pool and scrubbed at a few dark spots marring the interior wall.

My life changed in the next instant. In a moment of poor impulse control, I decided to throw the brush at my brother's head as he peacefully floated on his back. My throw wasn't hard and missed his head completely. Brian, almost four years my senior, jerked upright in the pool.

"I'm sorry. I didn't mean to throw it at you." I pleaded with my palms up.

At first he gaped at me, but then narrowed his eyes. I knew I was in big trouble. His seeking hand found the brush.

"Don't!" I shouted.

Brian whizzed the brush at my head with good aim. I attempted to dodge it, but without success. My two front teeth cracked in half on impact. Shocked, I watched as the pieces of my teeth drifted lazily to the bottom of the pool. They looked forlorn and odd.

With my hand cupped to my mouth, I stared at my brother. He had gone white under his tan. I wiped the small dribble of blood from my bottom lip, but not before a drop plopped into the perfectly clear water. The drop held its perfect shape for a moment and then slowly spiraled away.

Brian's mouth snapped shut and then he opened it again, "Come on, we have to get out of the pool."

He hurriedly waved me to the pool ladder. I shook slightly as I climbed back down the ladder. Once out of the pool, he bent down and gently lifted my top lip to look at my teeth. I stood there squinting my eyes against the sun as water ran down my legs and puddled in the green grass around my feet. Just inches apart, I watched Brian's dark blue eyes as he examined my mouth. He sucked in a deep breath and then blew out. I could smell the salami we had eaten for lunch on his breath.

"I'm a dead man." He let go of my lip and stepped back. "You can't tell Dad I did this." He squinted his eyes at me and pressed his mouth into a hard line.

"You think I don't know that already?" I frowned at him and put my hand on my hip. It insulted me that he thought I would tell Dad. "I'll just tell them my foot slipped on the ladder and my mouth hit the top step."

His face and shoulders relaxed. "Good idea. I'm sorry. I shouldn't have thrown it at you."

I shrugged and said, "I threw it at you first."

"You did. What were you thinking, moron?"

"Shut up!" I yelled. And then more quietly, "Who knows?"

I shook my head slightly and came back to the present moment. I remembered I hadn't cried one tear. When big things happened in my life I noticed I didn't emotionally react to them right away. I had learned to shut my emotions down.

I glanced back into the mirror. Brian had done me a favor. The veneers looked way better than my natural teeth. I had gone from beaver to beauty in that instant. Teeth inspection complete, I reached for the pink hand towel, wiped my mouth and quickly put the towel back on the rack. It was Saturday, my favorite day. I ate breakfast later, wore sweats, and enjoyed the freedom to do whatever I wanted. I happily thought about walking to Rebecca's house.

I stepped into my small bedroom humming to myself. I sat on the floor and pulled my running shoes out from under the bed.

"Jessie!" Dad snarled from the bathroom.

I froze, fingers holding my shoelaces, and stared at my short, unpolished nails. Heart pounding, I finished tying my shoes and rose. With dread, I realized Dad was blocking my exit path. My stomach muscles tightened as I walked into the narrow hallway toward the bathroom and stood in the doorway. Dad stood by the sink. His bald head made him seem taller than six feet. His cold dark eyes fixed on mine. As soon as he saw me, he jabbed his finger toward the white sink.

"Get over here. Did you leave this in the sink?" he demanded.

Stepping closer, I considered the white, normally spotless sink. It was marred with blue toothpaste spit. I hadn't wiped it out when I finished brushing my teeth.

"Do you think I'm your maid? That I enjoy wiping up your spit?" he said.

His body trembled, his hand clenched at his side. I studied my feet. I had learned from past mistakes not to make direct eye contact, as it made him angrier. Or maybe the look on my face did it?

"No, you're not my maid. I will clean it up," I said, hoping to placate him.

Too late. He was already in a righteous rage. Righteous from his viewpoint, as he spent at least two hours a day cleaning our small ranch-style home. He grabbed my shoulders and pushed me against the bathroom wall. My back and head thudded hard.

His face barely an inch away from mine, "I'm so sick of you," he said, spitting the words between his gritted yellow teeth.

His stale coffee breath washed over my face. His fingers encircled my throat, but he wasn't squeezing...yet. My head felt fuzzy, but I stared back into his hateful eyes.

"I'm so tired of picking up after you. I can't wait until you're out of this house," he hissed.

Mom rushed into the bathroom.

"What're you doing?" She grabbed Dad's hands and tore them away from my throat. She stared at him with eyes wide, and her mouth hanging open.

The insanity drained from his eyes with Mom's appearance. "She's looking at me like I'm a pig."

"Do you blame her?" Mom glared at him.

How right. You are a pig. Good. He'd received my subliminal messages. I was not the problem, he was. I took my chance and slid out of the bathroom, dashed to the front door and ran. Mom could deal with him.

"Jessie!" She called after me, but I didn't turn around. She offered me no comfort.

I jogged through our neighborhood, past Rebecca's house. I needed to calm down first. Anger boiled within me. I sprinted down the street trying to relieve the burning sensation in my chest.

Why did he hate me so much? Maybe he knew I hated him. He deserved my hate as he had done everything possible to earn it. Obligation was not enough, not by a long shot, to make me love him.

Slowing to a jog again, I turned back toward Rebecca's house, inhaling the damp smell from the woods and stream that bordered our subdivision. I released a long breath and began to walk past the houses, catching the smell of fabric softener venting from a dryer into the outside air. I loved that smell. It made me imagine the families in those houses peacefully folding their laundry and going about their predictable days. Boredom would be fantastic. Eventually, the mild fall air and the pretty red and gold leaves on the trees soothed me.

With a sense of relief, I approached Rebecca's. The quiet, always watchful girl I was at home didn't exist at Rebecca's. Here I could be a loud, giggly teenager. I went into their garage and knocked softly on the door.

"It's Jessie," I called out as I opened the door. The neat kitchen was empty, but I could smell something chocolate in the oven. Baking brownies were the best smell in the world. I shut the door behind me and headed to Rebecca's room.

"Rebecca?" I called. Her bedroom door was slightly ajar. She lay on the thick, cream shag rug listening to her phone.

"I love Saturday so much," she said, looking up at me.

I settled on the floor next to her. "Me too." I sighed.

She sat up and studied my face. "What's wrong?"

"Oh, you know, just your normal Saturday choking session." I pushed my emotions down. I couldn't allow myself to get upset. If I did, I would scream and howl like an animal.

"You have to report him," Rebecca said. "Tell the police or school, something."

I shook my head. "I know, but it won't do any good. His fellow officers won't believe me. He'll put on his I'm-struggling-with-a-teenager face, and then I'll look like the problem child. They did nothing last time I called them, and Dad pretty much threatened to kill me if I called them again."

"Please. We could talk to my mom. She would know how to handle it."

"No, please don't." I panicked. "I would be so embarrassed if people knew about my family. I couldn't bear it."

"I don't know. This is bigger than being embarrassed." She lowered her gaze to the floor.

"Rebecca, please. Swear to me that you will not tell your mom."

I studied her downcast eyes. She had been my best friend for as long as I could remember. She was the only person who really knew what my home life was like. I feared she wouldn't make this promise.

"I don't know what to do," she said.

The thought of her mom contacting my parents or school made my stomach turn. I believed Dad when he said he would kill me if I ever told anyone again.

Rebecca's mom called to us from the kitchen. "Girls, I made brownies, come have some."

As we stood up, I mumbled, "Saved by a brownie."

She half-smiled at me in response. "Come on, let's go before my dad takes them all."

I hung out with Rebecca most of the day. We lay on her rug, read magazines, listened to music, and talked about Harry Styles and his innate hotness.

"I love your room. I wish mine looked like this," I said.

"What do you like about it?" She turned on her side to look at me.

"I love the robin-egg blue walls, your pretty white quilt... and of course, this fabulous rug. It gives me something to aspire to," I said.

"I'm sure you'll get there," Rebecca said.

Rebecca's house was beautiful. I belonged there; it was one of the few places I was completely comfortable.

At five pm, I grudgingly gathered myself from the floor. "I have to go back to the dungeon now."

"Okay, call or text if you need anything," she said.

"I'm sure he'll be on his best behavior now to appease Mom." I hesitated in her doorway for a moment and her eyes met mine. "Please don't say anything to your mom."

She rubbed her forehead and didn't answer.

I sighed as I left her room. Her mom talking to or reporting my parents made my scalp tingle and fear run down my spine. Something like that would put both of my parents over the edge. I pushed the thought from my mind and shook my head. I wouldn't and couldn't think about that again without going crazy.

At least Brian would be home by now. As I entered the house, Dad and Mom were watching football. My gaze flicked over them briefly, but they both ignored me.

I plopped down on a barstool next to Brian in the kitchen.

His sibling sense kicked in. "What's wrong?"

"Another Dad attack this morning."

"What! Why? What did he do?" His eyes moved over my face and neck. Our childhood had made us closer than most siblings. Surviving our parents had united us.

"I left blue toothpaste spit in the sink. Apparently, choking me was an appropriate punishment," I said.

His face flushed red and his hand on the kitchen counter clenched into a fist.

"I would love to beat the shit out of him, so he could have a taste of his own medicine," he spat.

"Me too. Just make sure I'm around to see it when you do." We smirked at each other. That day would come, and I couldn't wait. Brian was bigger than Dad now. The thought was like a warm fuzzy blanket wrapped around me.

"Are you guys ready for dinner?" Mom said in her fake cheery voice as she walked into the kitchen. She opened one of the seventies-era brown cabinets, grabbed the plates and placed them on our ugly light orange countertops. As if the occupants of the house weren't depressed enough, the décor added to it.

Dinner consisted of oven-baked chicken, garlic bread and green beans. Brian and I ate dinner at the kitchen bar, while Mom and Dad sat at the dining room table. Five minutes into the meal, Brian had cleaned his plate and was eying mine.

"Are you going to eat your chicken?" He quickly glanced over his shoulder to see if Mom or Dad was paying attention.

"No, go ahead." It bothered me that he was still hungry.

"Thank you, sis."

He picked up my plate and slid the remaining contents onto his. Mom had been a chubby kid, so she tended to serve small portions. Brian could easily eat two chicken breasts, but Mom only gave him one. She didn't want either one of us to get a little fat on our bones. I ran a lot to relieve stress. Combined with our diet, it had made me thin and athletic.

After dinner, Brian and I went into the living room to watch TV. We sat on the floor with our knees hugged to our chests and our thin t-shirts stretched across our backs. I looked over at him and smiled. We always sat on the floor like this.

No more than five minutes had gone by when Dad yelled from the kitchen, "Kids, turn the TV down!"

I shook my head. What a prick. Sighing, I turned it off; it was more comfortable for us in our rooms anyway. The volume always had to be so low we couldn't hear it. God forbid he be reminded we were in the house.

I knew Dad wished we didn't exist at all.

CHAPTER 8

BRIAN

The high school halls were lit with a gray, gloomy light coming from the windows at each end. I felt the same way.

"Brian, I'm fine," Tracey said. I had asked three times before I got an answer. My arm gently rested on her shoulders.

"Okay, I just want to make sure." I squeezed her shoulder and anxiously watched her walk into class.

Frowning, I stared at the black and white tile floor and made my way to shop class. It would be good to have something occupy my mind. I sat down at the big table with the dull black counter.

Coach Wilson, our shop teacher, came strolling in dressed in his typical golf shirt and khakis, but today his wife followed behind him.

"Hey kids, I've got a special guest for you today. My wife, whom you may call Mrs. Wilson, has volunteered to work with us."

I nodded at her. I did know her, since she sometimes showed up at football practice to talk with Coach.

She seemed a little nervous— her hand shook slightly as she unpacked her large, black multi-pocketed bag.

"Mr. Wilson and I thought you might enjoy learning how to make some jewelry in class," she said as she arranged her stuff. "I've brought some beads, pendants, leather straps and other odds and ends. Come on up here and take a look." She motioned for us to join her.

I hustled over, maybe I could make something for Tracey. I scanned the items on the table and quickly zeroed in on two silver pendants shaped like wheels with five spokes.

I picked them both up and studied them in my hand. "What are these?" I held them out so Mrs. Wilson could see them.

"Good pick, those are Hindu symbols that mean seeking balance."

Seeking balance. I liked that. I could make a bracelet for Tracey with this cool pendant and the leather straps. And since I had two, I could make one for Jessie too.

"Is it okay if I take both of these?" I asked.

"Of course, I brought them for you guys," she said.

"Thank you," I took them back to my desk. They were smooth and heavy in my hand. I touched one of the spokes and slowly spun the wheel against my palm. I pictured the finished product in my head.

I went over to our supplies and rummaged around for thin leather straps I could loop around the pendant.

Mr. Wilson came up behind me as I looked. "So, what are you going to make?"

"I thought I could make bracelets for Tracey and Jessie with these," I said.

"Good idea, that should make the girls happy," Coach said. "Let me show you how to cut and measure out the leather for the straps."

I rubbed my right fist into my left palm. I couldn't wait to give the finished bracelet to Tracey.

CHAPTER 9

JESSIE

Home sucked, but my time at school made up for it. I couldn't stop smiling. I attempted to rein my lips in from their permanent smile while I opened my locker. Alex appeared behind me and placed his chin on my shoulder, his cheek next to mine.

"Hey," I said.

"You're going to Ally's house tonight, right?" he said.

"You know it." Our bubble gum breath mingled.

His hand slipped to my waist as he started to pull away. "I can't wait." He gave my hip a squeeze and headed to his class.

I floated to Mrs. Palmer's office with the feel of Alex's hand still tingling on my hip. We had shared a few quick kisses, but tonight we would have some privacy! My whole body buzzed at the thought. I wondered if this was what it felt like to be drunk? If Alex disappeared from my life now, I would suffer from withdrawal. Lovesick. I knew what it meant.

We had worked out a meeting at Ally's house. The details came together perfectly. Ally and Topher had just started dating, and Ally lived a few doors down from him. When her parents left for dinner, the boys would come over. All things had aligned for a fantastic evening.

I had barely settled in the office before Mrs. Palmer called out for me.

"Jessie?"

"Yes?"

"Could you come here please?" she asked.

"Sure." I walked over to the doorway of her office.

Mrs. Palmer gazed up at me. "Come in. I wanted to set up some time for us to talk."

"Okay," I said.

"How about we talk every Tuesday when you're here?" she asked.

"Sounds good," I replied.

"Perfect. Of course, you can pop in my office anytime if you need to." She made a note to her calendar.

"Thanks. I do have some questions. I googled 'out of body experience' and this information came up and said it could be related to post traumatic stress or personality disorders."

She motioned for me to take a seat. "I understand why you would want more information. Any disorder can be scary, but hopefully with the right treatment it can be managed or cured."

"Are personality disorders curable?" My voice shook. I cleared my throat.

"There are different kinds of personality disorders, ranging from mild to severe. Remember when I mentioned I volunteer at the Veterans Association hospital?"

I nodded.

"I volunteer to help soldiers deal with their feelings after being in combat. Your mirror episode is similar to symptoms they experience."

"Seriously? I have something soldiers get?"

"Possibly. You haven't been in combat, but you may have been in other stressful situations."

Oh, but I had been in combat. Combat with my own father, but I wasn't going to share that information.

"For example, as children if we have a parent or significant person in our lives who is unpredictable, emotionally or physically abusive, our minds separate from the situation. It's like you aren't paying attention, but more so. It's called dissociation." Mrs. Palmer watched my face as she talked.

"That sounds weird," I said.

"Can you tell me what happened before your last episode? Did anything upsetting occur?"

"Um…Dad and Brian got into a fight," I said.

"It's stressful when two people you love fight," she said.

I snorted, "I don't love my dad."

"Oh, okay." She seemed surprised at my admission.

She sat there in silence, waiting for me to elaborate. I hated that. It was so effective at making me talk. I crossed and uncrossed my legs.

"I don't know…my dad is an asshole and yells a lot. It seems like he is always ready to lose his temper." I took a deep breath and fidgeted in my seat. The conversation had rapidly gone a direction I didn't want it to go.

Mrs. Palmer looked concerned. "Does your father just yell? Or does he get physical as well?"

Oh crap. The last thing I needed was school looking into my home life further. My Dad would really kill me. I laughed nervously. "No, he just yells a lot, but it's still scary."

Mrs. Palmer was a perceptive adult. I tried to avoid them.

"I could contact your parents and let them know how these fights at home are affecting you. I could ask them to come in, and we could all chat together," she suggested.

"Um, I don't think we need to do that. I'm sure I'm fine. It's no biggie," I said. I slumped in my chair, but there was nowhere to hide.

"I'm sure your parents would want to know how it's affecting you. They probably don't realize. I'll reach out to them. It'll be fine," she said. "Okay," I mumbled. My head spun as I stood up to leave. "Walking dead girl" would be my new name.

CHAPTER 10

JESSIE

The bad school day forgotten, Ally and I pretended to casually loaf on the sofa as her parents got ready to leave for dinner. I wanted to pace back and forth and scream at them to leave already, for God's sake.

Ally's parents came into the family room a few moments later to talk to us before they left.

"Okay girls, we're going to take off now. Pick up any messes you make in the kitchen and remember not to have any additional friends over." Her mom looked at us with brows raised.

"I know the rules, Mom." I just nodded agreeably. I was an unrepentant liar where parents were concerned.

As soon as the front door shut, we ran to the bathroom to put on make-up and brush our hair. As a last touch, I squirted perfume up in the air. It settled onto my hair and skin like a soft perfumed cloud.

The guys must have been watching for Ally's parents to leave because only five minutes passed before we heard their tapping on the sliding-glass door.

"They're here!" My voice squeaked. We stared at each other and flapped our arms in a panic.

"Okay, calm down. Just let them in."

"Good idea."

The cold outside air clung to them as they came through the door. Their eyes were bright. Maybe it was the secretive nature of our meeting.

I stood there for a minute not knowing what to do.

Finally, Ally broke the ice. "Let's go hang out in the family room."

We followed her into the family room, where I clicked her smartphone into the player and started going through her playlist. Bruno Mars's soulful voice filled the room with "If I Knew," one of my favorite songs.

"I love this song," I said.

"Yeah? I haven't heard it before," said Alex. He cocked his head to the side.

I sat down next to him on the couch and he leaned over to kiss me, his lips still cool from the walk. I didn't want to make out in front of Ally and Topher, but Alex didn't appear to mind. His lips were soft and fuller than I expected. The peach fuzz on his upper lip pressed into my lips. He pulled me into his lap, and I melted into him. I forgot anyone else in the room. One song after another played as we kissed.

His hand caressed my back and timidly skimmed over my butt. One arm held me close to him as his hand made its way to my stomach. He pushed up my shirt a little and lay his hand flat on my stomach. With a mind of its own, my hand removed his.

He moved back and we broke apart. I probably looked like a dazed suckerfish with my lips extended.

"Sorry, too fast?"

I blushed and nodded. I enjoyed this, but I was hesitant as well.

"Do you hear this song?" he said.

It took a minute to defog my brain. "Crazy for You" by Madonna.

"Yeah, Ally likes eighties music."

"This song reminds me of you." His fingers gently stroked my jawline.

I didn't know what to say, so I caressed his face and kissed him again. I snuggled my head under his chin and tried to process what he'd said. His openness surprised me.

From the safety of his chest I said, "So, you're crazy about me?" I chuckled.

He hugged me tighter in response.

"So, besides football, what do you like to do?" I asked.

"I run track in the spring," he said.

"Really? I'm going to run track too. That'll be so fun."

"Yeah, bet you'll look great in those tiny shorts." He laughed.

I cringed. References to my butt embarrassed me. Everything embarrassed me.

"Are you doing anything else besides track?" He said.

"Yeah, I tried out for the school choir and made it. Me and Kristi are both in it."

"That's cool. I didn't know you could sing," he said.

"Yep, like a bird," I said.

Alex laughed. "You're funny too. I really like that about you."

"Thank you," You're hot, which is what I like about you, but I kept that little gem to myself.

Ally appeared wide-eyed in the family room. "My mom and dad are pulling in the driveway. You guys have to go."

I've never seen anyone move so fast. Alex bolted off the couch and sped to the back door. He gave me a quick kiss and then he and Topher disappeared into the darkness of the backyard. I kept watching the spot where they disappeared. Had it been a dream? One minute he'd kissed me, and the next he was gone.

Ally and I ran for her bedroom, smoothed our hair into place and rubbed the makeup off our faces. By the time her mom opened the door, we were sitting on the floor watching music videos on YouTube.

"Honey, you left the music on pretty loud. Please remember to turn it off," she said.

"Oh, sorry Mom," Ally said as we both regarded her mother with wide-eyed, innocent faces. Her mom waved at us and said goodnight.

"We're so good; we pulled that off no problem," Ally said. We mimed a silent scream.

"So how was the kissing with Mr. Alex Corbin?" she asked as we lay side by side on her king bed.

"Fantastic!"

She rolled toward me and bumped my shoulder. "Wow, he has the looks and the moves; kudos to him."

"How about Mr. Topher Morris?" I asked.

"It's obvious he's a seasoned pro."

I laughed. "Why do you think that?"

"He's good at it and based on the roving hands, he's ready for more. How were the hands on your end?" She leaned into me to convey the seriousness of her question.

"His hands were on my END!" We both giggled. "Mostly he kept his hands nicely on my back, only occasionally drifting down to my butt," I said.

"Well, your butt is lovely. How about mine? Do you think it's grab-worthy?" She rolled over to show me her pajama-clad butt.

"Of course it is. Why? Didn't he grab it?"

"Yep, first thing. I just wanted your assessment."

I clamped my hand over my mouth to muffle the sound of my laughter. We went on to discuss the merits of their butts. My stomach hurt from laughing so hard. "Oh, my God, we have to stop."

She held her hand over her mouth as she yawned, "Yeah, let's call it a night." She clicked off her bedside lamp and I settled in under her comforter. I hugged myself in the dark. Tonight had been so fun. As I drifted off to sleep, I wondered if I was ready for more than kissing.

CHAPTER 11

JESSIE

The muddy green water of the lake was cool, but I swam frantically, barely aware of the temperature. Heavy cloud cover blocked the sun. My rapid breath rebounded off the water. The smell of mud, moss and fish filled my nostrils. Dad thrashed in the water, swimming after me. I chanced a look back at him. His dark eyes focused on me. I could see the happiness in them. The joy evident on his face as he hunted me. I knew if he caught me, he would kill me. Who was this man? Why was he my dad?

I couldn't see the shore, and he was gaining on me. The sense of impending doom overtook me. I didn't think I could outswim him.

His hand clamped tightly around my ankle, grinding my bones. I started to scream and kick hard to loosen his grip. As I went under, I sucked in lake water.

My foot connected with my bedroom wall, and I awoke from the dream with a gasp. I sat up and rubbed my aching toes and foot. My heart pounded. Soaked in sweat, I flopped back down on my bed and took deep breaths. Unfortunately, nightmares made frequent appearances and the lake dream constituted a particularly bad, recurring one. I looked around my room and noted my closed bedroom door. The carefully arranged toys, stray Legos and stuffed animals on my floor were undisturbed. I'd booby-trapped the floor, not wanting Dad coming into my room with me unaware. I listened for sounds in the rest of the house to determine who was awake. I could hear Mom's light step on the kitchen floor. Luckily I didn't hear the radio playing oldies in the back bedroom, a telltale sign my dad was up.

I dragged myself to the kitchen to start my day with bran cereal. As I chewed, I slowly started to wake up. I thought about last night's drama. It had probably caused the dream.

Dad had come home late and drunk, which led to a fight with Mom. I stood still in the middle of my bedroom and listened to them fight. My legs twitched as adrenaline flowed through my body. Baby crawled under my bed and cowered. Brian knocked briefly and then let himself in. His worried face mirrored my own.

Dad yelled, "Did you know the school counselor left a message today, that she wants us to come in and talk about Jessie?"

"No, did she say why?" Mom asked.

"No, but I can just guess it's about some bullshit Jessie made up to get me in trouble," he yelled again.

"Calm down and stop shouting. We have no idea why she wants us to come in," Mom said.

"Where's Jessie?" Dad snarled.

Brian pushed me out my bedroom door. "Run."

I sprinted for the sliding glass door that led to the back yard. Five steps later, I heard the slam of the bedroom door. He was too close. I prayed, 'God, please help me. God, please help me.'

"Brian, fucking move," Dad said.

Brian bought me two steps and God did help me. God had made me fast, given me my brother and my intuition. I was meant to survive, I knew it. There was something else for me in this life.

Dad rounded the corner into the kitchen as I jerked open the sliding glass door. Barefoot, I dashed into the neighbor's yard. A short cut to Rebecca's house. Dad followed me into the backyard, Mom close behind him.

"Jessie, come back here now!" he bellowed into the night air. I could see he only wore underwear. What the hell was wrong with him? I had barely made it out in time. My stomach turned, and I puked into the bushes.

Darkness had fallen, so he didn't see me hiding. I spit and then wiped my mouth with my hand.

"Get into the house! Do you want everyone to think you're crazy?" Mom asked.

She shooed him back inside. Now what? I couldn't go back home. Not until his drunk ass passed out. Rebecca's, I would have to go there. I didn't have shoes and the ground was cold. I cut through backyards and tiptoed into Rebecca's garage. I knew there would be shoes by the backdoor. Wearing a pair of her old tennis shoes, I knocked softly.

Rebecca's mom came to the door.

"Jessie? What's wrong?" She frowned.

"Hi, I'm sorry, I know it's late, but I need Rebecca to show me how to do this algebra problem. If you don't mind?"

"No, of course not. Is everything okay?"

"Yep, math just sucks for me." Lying was effortless.

"Okay," she said. "She's in her room."

I took off the shoes I had just put on. I could see doubt on her face, but she accepted my excuse. I called out to Rebecca as I neared her door.

"What's wrong?" She sat up quickly, brow furrowed.

"Same old crap. Dad's drunk," I said.

"Do you want to stay here for the night?" she said.

"No, but I may need to pretend to leave and then sneak back in. I'll let him pass out before I go back," I said.

"Okay. I don't know how you stand this," she sighed.

"I don't have any other options. Isn't it amazing how my dysfunctional parents found each other and decided to have kids so they could scar them for life? Do people really not get that they're a mess?" I said.

"Seriously, it makes me see the reasoning behind controlled populations," she said.

"Let's move to China," I said.

We both laughed quietly. Humor was the only way to survive my life.

I didn't dwell on nightmares. I didn't think about my home life. Once I left the house, I left the drama there, for the most part. The only peace I enjoyed existed outside my home. I tried not to spoil it, but worry did creep in.

My hands scrubbed my face. One thought circled in my mind. Dad became more violent with each drunken episode. If he caught me, he would kill me. Mom wouldn't be able to stop him. Why didn't she see it?

CHAPTER 12

JESSIE

The next few months flew by, mainly due to my happiness with Alex. As I stood in front of my locker, one of the school's holiday decorations, a green, glitter-covered Christmas tree, fell over right in front of it. I picked it up and flipped it over to see if sticky putty clung to the back. It did, so I pressed the tree to my locker. I couldn't believe the holidays were right around the corner. Since we attended a Christian school, we celebrated Christmas. None of that 'Seasons Greetings' stuff.

A flutter of nerves flew through my stomach like tiny birds. Trying out for and making the choir had seemed like a good idea, but I hadn't really thought about the fact that singing in front of the entire school was part of the deal. I hated this nervous feeling. The holiday assembly took place today.

I shut my locker and took a deep breath to steady myself. Bottom line, I didn't care if it was uncool; I loved to sing. One thing I really liked about myself was that I didn't care what other people thought of me…unless I loved them.

Next up was my free class. Mrs. Palmer came out of her office as I entered.

"Hey Jessie, are you ready to chat?" she asked.

"Sure."

"How have you been?" she said, settling into her chair.

"I'm good," I said.

"Are you ready for the holidays?"

"Not really. I need to buy my parents something," I said.

"I know, I'm not ready either. Too much procrastination on my part," she said.

I kept my gaze lowered.

"I've called your home several times and left messages, but your parents haven't returned my calls."

"I don't think they'll return your calls," I said quietly. "They just avoid things they don't want to deal with."

"Well that approach isn't going to work in this situation. I do need to talk with them so you can get the care you need," she said in a peeved tone. "How are things going at home?"

"The same, Dad fights with me, Mom and Brian." I shrugged.

"How're you coping? Do the fights cause any out of body experiences?"

"I guess. I've had a few. It's awful," I mumbled.

"We should—"

She started to say more, but I blurted, "What if I end up like them?" It was my greatest fear.

"You won't," she said confidently.

"How do you know?"

"Do you know how brave it is of you to come into my office and talk to me?"

"No."

"Most children are forced to come to counseling, but you came to me with a problem of your own accord. It's so mature for your age." She beamed at me like a proud parent.

"Oh," I said.

"The biggest reason why you won't be like them, is because you consciously don't want to be like them. Already at fourteen, you've made that choice," she said.

"Okay." Her words made me start to cry. Happiness glowed in my chest.

"I'm so impressed by you. You're wise beyond your years." Her eyes crinkled in the corners as she looked at me affectionately.

"Thanks." I blinked back the tears.

"I'm going to take some additional action to contact your parents, but I don't want you to worry," she said.

My stomach rose to my throat. "Please don't contact them. It will only make things worse. She won't change, and neither will my dad," I said.

"You don't know that for sure. They could change with some help."

A student knocked on the door. Mrs. Palmer glanced at them through the window. Blood drained from my face; I could feel the familiar numbness taking over.

"Could you wait to contact her? Until the holidays are over," I asked.

She sighed. "I don't know. It would be better for you to get the help you need sooner rather than later," she said.

"Please wait," I said again as I slid out the door. I stood outside her office for a minute to calm myself. I prayed she wouldn't contact them again. I pushed my panic down. Brian would help me figure something out.

I made my way to the choir room. We were rehearsing "Carol of the Bells" for the assembly. I loved the overlapping soprano and tenor verses. It sounded beautiful. We even rang heavy silver bells to accompany our voices.

I could hear the general pandemonium from the choir room before I reached the doors. Complete chaos reigned. I shuffled over to Kristi, who was already in her black robe.

"What's wrong? Your face is white," she said.

"Nothing's wrong. I'm fine." I had to shake this doomsday feeling. I forced a smile onto my face. "You look hot in your robe, by the way."

"Bite me. You have to wear it too," she said.

I chuckled and put my books under my chair. As I bent down, chills overcame me and I dropped into my chair. Thoughts of Mrs. Palmer escalating contact with my parents raced through my mind. I pulled my robe closer around me and searched for my candle.

"Have you seen it? I just had it and now I can't find it." I glanced under my chair and in the next aisle: nothing.

"How do you like my candle, baby?" Kristi said. I turned and noticed her candle jutting out from between her thighs.

I laughed. "Very attractive. Good thing it's an LED candle."

She laughed and retrieved her candle. I bent over to look under the row of chairs in front of us.

"It's in your bag, dumb ass," Kristi said as she handed it to me.

"This from the girl with a candle between her legs," I said.

"Are you sure you're okay? You look scared or something." Her eyes searched my face.

"I'm a little chilled. I hope I'm not getting sick," I said.

We lined up in the right order to fill the risers in the gym. The line of kids looked like a wiggling black snake. No one stood still for more than ten seconds.

"Everybody quiet down! Line up at the door now," yelled Miss Stevens, our choir director. As she zoomed by me on her way to the front of the room, I distinctly heard her say 'Jesus Christ' under her breath. I was quite confident Jesus wasn't going to help with this situation.

We filed into the hallway for the short walk to the gymnasium. The entire student body sat in the bleachers. The choir line stopped in front of the double doors as Miss Stevens ensured we were ready to go. As soon as the first person entered the gym, the entire choir started to sing.

Hark how the bells, Sweet silver bells,
All seem to say, Throw cares away
Christmas is here, Bringing good cheer,
To young and old, Meek and the bold.

As I entered the gymnasium, I heard our voices expand to fill the much larger space. The silver bells rang, the sound shimmering outward. The sopranos sang, 'Merry, merry, merry, merry Christmas', while the tenors sang the main chorus. The candles and our strong young voices created a warm holiday net over our entire student body. For a moment, I forgot my fears.

Merry, merry, merry, merry Christmas, (Merry Christmas)

As we sang, I looked over to the freshman section of the gym. They didn't look too terribly bored. We went on to sing several more songs, and then Miss Stevens gave us the signal to stop.

She picked up the microphone. I cringed for her. Why did I get embarrassed for other people?

"Thank you all for listening so attentively while we sang. The choir and I love those songs, and we hope you enjoyed them too. Now, though, I would like you all to join in as we sing some classics."

She raised her arms to signal us to begin. Maybe being in the choir wasn't such a good idea? Embarrassment overwhelmed me with this public display. We began with "Over the River."

Again, I scanned the sections of students broken up by grade. I grinned when I spotted my brother with his head thrown back singing vigorously with his buddies. They were all shoulder to shoulder and swaying with the music. Tracey sat behind him, laughing. Of course, the whole senior class looked at them. Idiots. They didn't care what anyone thought; they were seniors. I loved their freedom and silliness.

"Jingle Bells," was next and then "O Holy Night" for the last song. It surprised me that most of the students sang along, I sighed as the last notes died in the gymnasium. The entire gym remained quiet for a few seconds of magic.

Then the choir dispersed in all directions at once. I spotted Alex and moved toward him. Before I reached him, though, Amanda appeared, and gave him a hug. I stumbled, and something clicked in my head.

CHAPTER 13

THE OTHER

I stepped directly in front of the girl. "Why don't you stop embarrassing yourself? You're like a bitch in heat," I said.

Her mouth hung open.

"Jessie!" Alex's eyebrows shot up. He reached out his hand to stop my forward movement.

"I don't think Alex minds. Do you mind Alex?" Amanda said.

"Amanda, drop it." He grabbed my hand before I could smack her. She would regret her interest in Alex. He pulled me toward the back stairwell.

"What's going on? You never act like that," he asked. He wrinkled his forehead and studied my face.

I pulled my hand free. "She obviously has the hots for you, and I'm sick of her," I said.

He took a step away from me.

"Make sure she knows not to touch you again. Do you understand?" I said.

"Uh, I...I will tell her," he stammered.

"Good, do that." This whole scene bored me. "I have to go." I turned to walk away.

"Don't you want to talk about seeing each other during the break?" he extended his hand toward me, palm up.

"Not really," I said.

CHAPTER 14

BRIAN

My eyes watered from the bright winter sunlight. I was so stoked it was officially winter break. I squeezed Tracey's hand as we walked to my car in the school parking lot. She gazed up at me. She seemed better lately, more like how she used to be.

As we got closer, I noticed Jessie.

"What's up? Why didn't you take the bus?"

She picked at the sleeve of her choir robe but didn't answer me.

Tracey put a hand on her shoulder. "Are you okay?" She peered into Jessie's face.

"I don't feel well. Will you take me home?"

"Okay, but stop acting weird," I said.

Tracey smacked my shoulder.

"What?" I said, meeting her glare.

"She said she doesn't feel well." Tracey gave me her squinty-eyed look, then draped an arm around Jessie and guided her to the car door. "Boys, they just don't get it," she said as she squeezed Jessie's shoulder.

We were quiet on the ride home. Jessie curled into a ball in the backseat and went to sleep.

"What do you think is bugging her?" I quietly asked.

She shook her head. "I don't know, maybe she had a fight with Alex."

"I'll kill that kid," I said.

"You know you can't say that about every boy Jessie likes."

"Yes, I can. I'm her brother and that's my job." I puffed out my chest and banged my closed fist against it.

Tracey rolled her eyes and sighed. Maybe I was being annoying. We pulled into her driveway.

"I'll pick you up tonight at seven." I gave her a quick kiss and got back into the car.

Moments later, I pulled into our driveway and turned the car off. I looked in the backseat.

"Jessie, we're home. Wake up," I said.

She sat up and rubbed her eyes. "What time is it?"

I frowned. "It's 2:45, moron. I just brought you home."

"Why did *you* bring me home?" she asked.

"I don't know. You tell me. You were the one waiting by my car," I said.

She looked disoriented as we walked into the house. Kind of like the guy who'd gotten a concussion during a football game last year.

Awareness dawned on her face. "Oh, before I forget. Mrs. Palmer said she would call mom again or something to talk about our home situation."

"Are you kidding me? Dad will completely lose his shit again if the school calls."

"Do you think he remembers when they first called?" she asked.

"Probably not, since he was so drunk, but the results will be the same—him wanting to kill you. You have to stop talking to that counselor."

"I can't avoid her. I'm her office worker third period," she said.

She sat down at the kitchen counter while I scrounged the kitchen for food. I ate a banana due to the lack of other choices.

"How did this even get started in the first place?" I said, swallowing.

"I haven't been feeling well lately. It seems like something is wrong in my brain."

"What?" I studied her pale face. "I could have told you that."

"Shut up!" she yelled.

"What do you mean, something is wrong with your brain?"

"I don't know, it's hard to explain." She groaned. "I don't remember how I got to your car today."

"What? How do you not remember coming to my car today?" I asked. "Didn't you just walk there after the assembly?"

"I don't remember walking there!" she shouted. She started to cry. A loud cry with her mouth hanging open and snot running from her nose. There's nothing worse than a crying girl.

"Okay, okay." I held my hands up, attempting to calm her.

"Just forget it, I'm too tired to talk about it." She wiped her runny nose with the back of her hand.

I stood on the other side of the kitchen counter awkwardly. I didn't know what to do or say.

"We'll have to block the school's phone numbers on Mom's phone. I know all the office numbers. Then she'll never get the call."

"Good one." I was impressed.

"I just want to stop this nightmare. Make sure you get the mail every day and watch for a letter from school."

"I'll try, but I don't always get home first. And stop talking to the counselor too." I shook my head, and fear crawled up my back like a spider. I would protect my sister, no matter what.

CHAPTER 15

JESSIE

I lay down on my bed and snuggled Baby close to my chest. My phone dinged. *"Are u mad at me?"* read the text from Alex. I sat up in bed. Why would I be mad at him?

"No, y would I be mad?"

"Because Amanda hugged me."

When did Amanda hug him? I didn't see Amanda hug him.

"When?" I typed.

"?????? Right after the assembly."

What else did I not remember about today? Fear flowed through my body with every heartbeat.

"Right. No, I'm not mad." My mouth went dry as I typed the words. Something was seriously wrong with me.

We exchanged a few more messages about when we would see each other.

"Going to nap. Bad headache," I typed.

"K, feel better. Txt me when you get up."

My head throbbed as I lay back down. Baby licked my chin—my sweet girl, she was such a comfort. My head throbbed. I closed my eyes and welcomed the numbness of sleep.

The following weeks passed in a blur. Christmas Eve arrived faster than I imagined. It was fully dark as we pulled into the church parking lot. I loved Christmas Eve services, with the white lights strung on the trees surrounding the church. The lights glowed, breaking up the surrounding darkness. The cloudless sky showcased the bright stars;

I gazed up at them and inhaled the chilly air. It seemed pure and magical. I sensed unity in the stars, something that joined us all together. I wasn't always sure about what was taught in church, but this feeling I believed. The wholeness, the wonder and love of something much greater than me. We were all part of a larger whole, all linked together. I was sure of it.

I pushed the air out of my lungs and watched it swirl away in the frigid air. Brian and my parents entered the church while I hung back and stared at the sky. Sighing, I pulled my coat tighter around me and joined them.

At the door, a greeter handed me a candle with a cardboard circle around it. The dimmed lights, decorations and hushed atmosphere transformed the sanctuary. The scent of pine wreaths mingled with melted candle wax. Silver and gold decorations twinkled in the glow from the candles. Brian caught my attention with a small wave. I sat in between him and Mom.

Reverend White greeted the congregation and then asked us to take out our hymnals. As we began to sing, "The Hallelujah Chorus," I noticed Mom's off-key voice and winced. I could match tone by ear, but Mom couldn't, and she didn't read music. I looked around at our fellow parishioners to see if anyone else noticed.

I elbowed Brian and flicked my eyes toward Mom. He tilted his head to listen, then rolled his eyes and hung his head. We spontaneously started to sing off key as well. I increased my volume and we moved our heads side to side like we were really into it.

Mom frowned at us, then understanding dawned on her face.

"Oh hush, you two are terrible," she whispered while making a shooing gesture with her hand.

Brian and I shook with silent laughter. At least Mom had a sense of humor. A little entertainment made the service go by faster. I listened to the first five minutes of the sermon, then my mind started to wander. Brian's elbow brought me back to reality. He held out his lit candle to light mine. Candlelight filled the darkened sanctuary, projecting halos around everyone's heads. I wanted to freeze the moment, the peacefulness.

When we got home, I took off my church clothes and changed back into my sweats, then cuddled up in front of the fire and let my mind wander while the flames changed shape and color. My mind mostly wandered around thoughts of Alex, his cute smile, his sparkling blue eyes.

"Jess, come in here. I want to show you something," Dad called from the kitchen.

His friendly tone surprised me. Regardless, my stomach tensed as entered the room.

He was standing in front of the oven. "I want to show you how to make homemade hot chocolate. Grandma Taylor taught me to make it, and now it's your turn. It's way better than the packaged stuff."

He put a heavy silver pot on the stove. I stood back a bit, hesitant to stand right next to him. It was like being asked to approach a coiled snake.

"First you measure out the powdered cocoa." He spooned some into a glass measuring cup, then dumped it into the pot. "Next, add one third cup of sugar and mix the two together well. See?"

I stepped closer to him and peered into the pot to see the cocoa and sugar combined into a light brown mixture. I nodded. If he had ever acted this nice before, I didn't remember it.

"The next part is tricky. Pour just a small amount of milk into the pot and then mix it together. It will mix better that way. If you put too much milk the cocoa will ball together."

"Okay," I said.

"Once it's mixed well, slowly stir in the rest of the milk, set the burner to medium heat and just wait for it to warm. Don't stop stirring though or it will burn," he warned me.

We both stood there and watched as the mixture started to bubble. He continued to stir. The delicious smell of chocolate, sugar and warm milk floated toward my face. "It smells great," I said.

"It does." He looked pleased with himself. "It's ready. Go get Brian and Mom so they can have some too."

As I went to get Brian, I wondered if he was high on something to cause such a change in attitude. Moments later, we all sat around the family room with our mugs of hot chocolate, Brian made eye contact with me and lifted one brow in a silent question. I answered back with a subtle shrug. I had no idea where Dad's bout of niceness had come from. Holiday spirit maybe.

As I sipped my hot chocolate, I thought, wow, I learned something from my father. He had taught me one other thing, but I don't think he intended to. It was how to pretend you're the person people think you are.

The evening wound down and Mom and Dad went to bed. Brian and I sat on the couch. I watched TV and Brian read.

"What are you reading?" I asked leaning over his shoulder. He hunched over the book and read intently.

"*Rosemary's Baby*. Tracey read it and she thought I would like it." He chewed on a fingernail.

"Well, have fun with that bit of light reading." I shook my head and laughed quietly. An interesting book choice during Christmas.

"It's freaking me out," Brian said.

"Stop reading it then," I said.

"I can't. I have to find out what happens."

"I'm going to bed, good luck with that." I started to get up.

"Hey…sit up with me for a little bit?" He eyed me hopefully. "I don't want to read this by myself."

"Seriously?" I rolled my eyes, but I couldn't turn down that pathetic face. "Fine, but I may have to tell Tracey about this."

"Uh huh," he mumbled, already reading. He knew I would never embarrass him. The important thing about us—we had each other's backs.

I sat back down and started flipping through the channels. I wasn't focused on the TV but on how Dad had acted earlier today. What would our lives have been like if he had been kind and decent? Would I have been different? Unfortunately, he wasn't kind or decent, so I would become what he created.

CHAPTER 16

JESSIE

Two days later, Mom dropped me off at Alex's house so we could do our gift exchange. I practically bounced up to his front door in excitement.

"Hello Jessie," Mrs. Corbin said as she opened the door. "It's so nice to meet you."

Alex's dad waved at me from his armchair, then went back to reading the paper.

"Thank you, it's so nice to meet you." I extended the holiday serving tray toward her. "I made you all some Christmas cookies."

"I didn't know you baked," Alex said, appearing next to his mom. He opened the foil wrap and started grabbing cookies.

His mom playfully slapped his hand. "Stay out of those. We're going to eat soon." She beamed at him adoringly, just like I did. "Thank you, Jessie, for bringing cookies; how sweet of you. Now we have dessert."

"You're welcome." I rattled the bag I had brought with me. "Are you ready for your presents?" I asked Alex.

"Why don't you guys go in the family room and open your presents. The Christmas tree is in there," said Mrs. Corbin, gazing warmly at me.

As soon as we were out of sight, he picked me up and hugged me. "I've missed you so much."

"I know. Me too." I inhaled his scent. It was oxygen to me.

He knelt in front of the Christmas tree, pulling me down with him. He reached under the tree for a small box and excitedly handed it to me. "Ladies first."

I peeled back the heavy silver wrapping paper. It revealed a little black box and inside it a burgundy velvet box. My whole body flushed with nervousness. I gingerly opened it to see a delicate gold chain with a small, dimensional gold heart pendant. The gold heart also had a tiny diamond cushioned in its center.

"Oh Alex, I love it! It's beautiful."

"Do you? I'm so glad. I was nervous you wouldn't like it." He wiped his palms down the front of his jeans.

"I don't *like* it...I love it! Will you help me put it on?" I happened to glance at the back of the heart before I handed the necklace to him.

"It says 'First Love' on the back. Did you know that?" The question weighed heavy in the space between us.

"Of course. I bought it. It's true, you know." he said softly.

My eyes welled with tears and I wrapped my arms around him. I buried my lips and nose against his neck. Again, I inhaled his perfect guy scent. From the safety of his neck I murmured, "I love you Alex, so much." He pushed me gently away from him, so he could clasp the necklace around my neck. The necklace hung in a perfect V. I would cherish it always. I knew then I would keep this gift until I died, always treasured, no matter what happened between us.

"It looks great on you." He beamed as he leaned back to get a better view.

"My presents seem so silly compared to this one," I said.

"I'm sure they aren't."

I gave him the bigger box first. He opened it quickly and held up the blue, Italian wool sweater.

"Wow, it's super soft." He rubbed the fabric between his thumb and finger. "Nice."

"I thought it would look perfect with your blue eyes." "What do you think?" He laid the sweater against his chest.

"It matches perfectly," I said.

"Thank you." He reached for the smaller package and opened it. "*LUXE* cologne, I've never heard of this one."

"I must have smelled twenty different kinds of cologne. My nose wanted to go on strike it was so overstimulated," I said, grimacing. "Anyway, I liked this one the best."

He leaned over to give me a kiss. "Thank you, I really like both gifts."

We sat there and looked at each other. I never tired of looking at him.

"Let's sit on the couch. We'll be more comfortable," he said.

"Thank you again for the necklace. I love it."

I leaned into him and we kissed. It only took a few minutes of kissing before I succumbed to the familiar, almost gravitational pull of our bodies. I wanted to be as smashed together as possible. We couldn't get close enough. The urge was so strong; only the thought of his parents nearby kept me sane. All logical thought rapidly fled with desperation taking its place. Alex's hands discovered my body with increasing intensity.

As he moved his hand over my breast, I caught it and pulled it back down. "Your parents are in the next room," I whispered. Our noses touched, and Alex's warm breath bathed my face.

"I'm afraid they'll come in here." I scooted back from him, lifted my knees and hugged them close to my chest. "Wow that gets out of control fast." I trembled slightly.

"This is killing me." He jerked forward. I could see the muscle in his jaw tighten.

"I know, me too." I took in a deep breath of air to steady myself.

"Let's play cards, so we can cool down a little," I suggested.

"I don't want to cool down," he said. He did get up though, and grabbed a deck of cards.

"I'm sure Ally and I can pull off another hookup at her house," I said.

"Fantastic, I will talk to Topher." His eyes lit up and his mood improved.

Alex's mom came in to tell us dinner was ready. I thanked God that we were only playing cards.

"I hope you don't mind that I ordered Mariano's pizza and salad?" she asked me. "We've fed our relatives for days. I'm sick of cooking."

"No problem," I said. "Mariano's is my favorite pizza. I love the thin crust."

"And the saltiness, right?" she asked.

"Definitely."

Of course, you suck up to your boyfriend's mom, that's 'girlfriend 101', but I did already like her. Her demeanor was relaxed and calm, the kind of person who was comfortable in their own skin.

We all sat down in their warm, homey kitchen for dinner. Wide panels of hardwood covered the floor like an old saloon. The cabinets were the same maple-brown, golden color. What I couldn't see, but feel, was the warm, mellow happiness of the room. I watched as Alex talked and joked with his parents. They were open and loving. A natural ease existed between them. The whole scene played like a foreign movie to me. I had never experienced this type of relationship with my parents.

I started to reach for another piece of pizza but stopped and pulled my hand back. It was trembling. I picked up my napkin instead and wiped my mouth, hoping they hadn't noticed. What the hell was wrong with me? Suddenly, I recognized the feeling; it was longing. I wanted this life for myself so badly. I quietly and slowly took a deep breath and let it out, promising myself I would have a family like this someday.

CHAPTER 17

BRIAN

My hand rested on the orange kitchen counter while I waited for Mom to finish putting food into plastic containers. I shifted my weight from one foot to the other.

"Brian, take the dishes out to the car. Make sure you pack them in, so they don't turn over," Dad said.

He handed me the still warm dishes with lids, and I took them out to the trunk, annoyed. How in the hell was I going to keep these from sliding around and spilling everywhere? I stood there staring into the trunk. Beach towels! I could wrap the dishes in them. I mentally patted myself on the back.

On New Year's Day, we all packed into the car for the two-hour drive to see our grandmother. I dreaded it already. Dad would drink too much and make an ass of himself. No wonder Grandma hated him.

I shut the trunk and noticed Jessie seated in the backseat. Mom and Dad headed toward the car as well.

"Let me grab my phone." I jogged into the house and grabbed it off the kitchen counter.

As I got into the car, Dad stashed a twelve pack of beer on the seat beside him. Oh great, here we go again. I slumped in my seat and looked over at Jessie, pointing quickly to the front seat. She nodded her head slightly. yeah, she knew about the beer in the front seat. We had perfected our form of silent communication, much like men in the military.

Six beers later, Dad entered his happy phase of drunk. "Come on kids, let's sing row, row, row your boat. I'll start at one hundred!"

Rather than risk a beating, we started to sing along. We made it to ninety-two before he realized he couldn't drink beer and sing at the same time.

"All right, I'm calling for a refreshment break. Whoa, singing is thirsty work," he said, chuckling to himself. "Kids, do you want me to stop and get you a pop?" he asked.

"Nah, we're good. Thanks Dad," I answered for both of us. If he would just stay in this stage, I wouldn't care if he were drunk every day. He was nice at this stage. Forty-five minutes later, around the ninth beer, the ugly phase would begin.

I was relieved when Grandma's house came into view. Dad had grown quiet. Jessie and Mom got out of the car and went directly to the front door. I made my way to the back of the car to help Dad with the covered dishes and our bags.

I popped open the trunk and my stomach sank. During the drive, the macaroni casserole had slid free of the towels and spilled into the trunk. A little cheese sauce and a few macaroni were visible on the dark carpet.

Dad came around the car and stared into the trunk.

"Didn't I tell you to make sure the dishes didn't spill? This is a complete mess!"

He gritted his teeth and backhanded me in the mouth.

"Guess who'll have to clean it up? Me, of course, because you would do a half-assed job of it," he said.

I could taste blood in my mouth. The suddenness of the attack stunned me.

"Are you happy now? You've ruined our day."

I stood there like a stupid little boy every time he yelled at me. "Go get the paper towels out of the backseat."

My lip throbbed, and I must have stood there for a second too long. I started to back away from him. He grabbed the front of my shirt with both hands and pushed me backward.

"Get the paper towels, you idiot!" he yelled.

I stumbled back a few feet and fell.

The front door of the house opened, and Jessie streaked across the yard toward Dad. She ran fast and smooth like a cheetah. Not at all like her usual bouncy step.

She positioned herself between me and Dad.

"STOP! Don't you touch him again. Do you hear me?"

She turned to me and shrieked, "Brian, take him! You're stronger than he is! Take him now."

Paralyzed, I couldn't make myself get off the ground. The frozen grass melted under my hands as I stared at her in shock.

Dad stalked toward her. She lifted a long kitchen knife from her side.

With her teeth bared, she swung the knife. It sliced through the air. Dad jumped back to avoid the blade.

"Jessie!" he shouted.

She looked at him and sneered. "No. I'm not Jessie." Enraged, she swung the knife again. "Since you are such a subpar human being and father, now you will deal with me." Fearless and deadly serious, she stood her ground. Through gritted teeth, she said, "You will never touch either of them again. You got that, Dad?"

Her eyes never left his face. I had no doubt of her conviction.

Just then the front door opened, and Mom stepped out. "What's taking so long out here?" she asked.

Jessie straightened out of her defensive crouch and moved the knife to the side of her thigh.

I quickly got up and wiped off my pants. Mom conveniently overlooked me on the ground. Thanks Mom.

"Coming, just cleaning up a little spill," Dad said.

Really? It was a little spill now?

Dad shot Jessie a hateful glare. She, however, just sauntered back into the house like nothing happened. I walked over to the trunk to help him clean up.

"Go!" He swung his arm back like he would hit me again, but I dodged the blow.

Dazed, I stumbled into Grandma's house and collapsed at the kitchen table. When Dad came in, Jessie stood by the kitchen counter. She took the knife still clutched in her hand and slid it back into the wood block. She stared directly at Dad and tapped the handle of the knife with her finger. Without an ounce of fear, her eyes narrowed, and vertical lines appeared on each side of her mouth. She stood tall, her body stance ready to attack, like an alpha predator. She appeared to be reminding him of her threat. My mouth hung open. I had never seen an expression like that on anyone's face, let alone my sister's.

Dad pressed his mouth into a thin line. He gazed at her with his dull eyes. He yearned to beat the shit out of her, it was obvious. Mom, as usual, was oblivious to all.

A moment later, Grandma walked into the kitchen to check on dinner.

"Jessie, I didn't get my hug yet," she said as she opened her arms.

I held my breath.

"Of course," Jessie said as she leaned into Grandma's embrace, her demeanor sliding easily back to that of an innocent fourteen-year-old girl.

"I've missed you so much, you little doll." Grandma rubbed Jessie's back. "You're prettier every time I see you."

"Grandma?" Jessie sagged in her arms. Her hand reached up to the side of her head. She seemed confused. "Grandma, do you mind if I go lie down in your room? My head hurts."

"Of course, baby, go lie down." She held Jessie's shoulders slightly away from her body and studied her face. "You look pale. Do you feel sick?"

"Just a headache." Jessie left the kitchen and headed toward the bedroom. Dad started to follow her out of the kitchen.

"Lou?" Grandma said loudly. "Would you mind helping me get the serving tray down from the cabinet, please? I just can't reach up that high anymore." I knew she asked to prevent him from following Jessie.

It didn't stop me. I got up from the kitchen table and walked to Grandma's room. Jessie had laid down with the comforter pulled over her. I sat on the bed and tapped her arm. She looked up at me with her face scrunched up in pain.

"What the hell just happened outside?" I said.

"What?" she mumbled. "Go away. My head hurts." She pulled the comforter over her head.

Great. I sat there for a minute. "Jessie?" I prodded her shoulder, but she didn't respond. I gave up and went back into the kitchen.

Dad sat at the table with a cup of coffee in front of him.

I laughed to myself because I knew Grandma gave it to him without saying a word.

"Brian, let me have a look at you. You're such a handsome man. You look more like Grandpa every day." Her eyes filled with tears.

"I know. I miss him too," I said.

She put her soft hand under my jaw and turned my head to the side and then directly in front of her. "What happened to your lip? It's split."

I looked at her sweet, wrinkled face and her bright blue eyes and hesitated. I didn't want to lie to her. My hesitation must have tipped her off. Her eyes darkened with understanding.

Mom came into the kitchen and sat down.

"Mom, did you make—" she began.

"Lou, why is Brian's lip split?" Her strident tone of voice backed up her demand.

"That kid is always getting banged up in football." He took a sip of his coffee and tried to play it off as no big deal.

Grandma looked at me. "Brian?"

I looked over at Dad and said, "I'm done covering for you."

He shot back in his chair and started toward me. Grandma pulled a heavy frying pan from the stove and stepped around me.

"Don't you dare." She raised the pan with every intention of laying Dad out with it.

It was awesome.

Her mouth pressed into an angry line. "I would dearly love to smack your face with this pan right now." She glared at him. "What the hell is wrong with you? Answer me!"

Dad cringed like a rat caught in a trap, and Grandma slowly lowered the frying pan. It appeared to take a significant effort on her part to put it back down.

She turned to Mom. "Jan, I shudder to think what your father would have done in this situation. I'm glad he's not alive to witness this." Grandma whipped her hands up. "Why are you allowing this?" Mom wouldn't meet Grandma's eyes. "I don't know why you would put up with anyone hurting your children, especially their father," Grandma said.

Grandma's eyes laser-focused on Dad. "Lou, don't even try to deny you've hit the kids. And you're drunk…again, I might add."

"Now listen—"

"No, *you* listen to *me*. You will get your life together. Get your ass in rehab, move out of the house, but something needs to be done."

She let her words sink in. "Shame on you both. Jan, your behavior is worse than his."

"Mom, you're overreacting. Families fight occasionally," Mom said.

"Brian, how many times have you been hit?" Grandma looked at me expectantly with one hand on her hip.

I looked at Dad and then Mom. "Too many times."

Grandma brought the hammer down.

"This is going to stop. Do you hear me? If you don't address this, I will report you both to children's services," she said.

Dad's face turned with suppressed anger. He wouldn't act out here; he knew not to cross Grandma. I wished Mom had inherited some of her courage.

"Why does Jessie's head hurt?" She paused a second. "Oh my God, did you hit her too?" She advanced on Dad with her hand raised as though to smack him, but I stepped in front of her. Dad might lose control. She stopped, lowered her hand and took a deep breath. "I want the two of you gone. I can't stand to look at either one of you another minute."

"Mom, I'm not leaving here without my children. You can't just take over."

"Oh, yes I can. I will give you one week to make a change. If a change isn't in place, I will report you. I'll call the chief of police myself."

Dad motioned for Mom to get up. I stood protectively in front of Grandma. "Jan, let's go." He glowered at Grandma. "This isn't over," he said.

"I'm not a child, Lou. Don't you dare threaten me. Get out of my house!"

Mom hesitated, but Dad pulled her by the hand toward the front door.

I had to give props to Grandma. The tough old broad stood her ground. Something shifted within me. This fragile, old woman had commanded my dad like a general. I would never let Dad touch me or Jessie ever again. Jessie was right. I was strong enough to take him. The next time he hit me, I would hit him back with everything I had. It felt good to acknowledge it to myself.

Mom looked at me with her eyes tearing up. "Brian, we'll see you in a few days. I love you. Tell Jessie we love her."

I just stared back at her. Saying I loved them was something I didn't want to do. They left.

I hugged Grandma. "Grandma, you're awesome."

She sank into a kitchen chair. "Thank you, sweetie." She twisted her wedding band back and forth. "I'm sorry. I didn't want to believe it, but I suspected something. I could tell you were both afraid of your father. I prayed your mom would handle it. I realize today she's not capable of it."

"At least you spoke up. No one else has," I said.

Grandma just shook her head in response. "Your mother should have," she said with a sob. She covered her mouth with her hand and stared down at the dining room table.

I put my hand on her shoulder.

After a minute or two, she sat up and straightened her shoulders. "You go sit on the couch, and I'll get some ice for your lip. Maybe some turkey and stuffing smothered in gravy in a little while? I don't think it will hurt your mouth," she said.

"I don't care, it sounds too good." My stomach growled in response. I paused for a moment, hesitant to ask. "Why does she put up with him?"

"I don't know. Grandpa drank in your mom's early years, but he stopped by the time she was eight or nine. He certainly never hit your mother, nor was he mean." She sat quietly for a minute. "Sometimes women marry men that remind them of their fathers. Your mom did see her father drink." She rubbed her forehead. "I don't understand why she lets this go on. I'm sorry you and Jessie have been put through this. If your dad doesn't straighten up, we'll figure something out. I don't want the two of you to ever feel like you don't have anyone to depend on."

I clenched my teeth to push my emotion down.

"I know we have to go back to school in a few days; besides that, I don't know." I didn't trust myself to say more. I went into the living room and sat on the couch. What a relief to be here. I'd let Grandma baby me for a few days. I debated whether I should mention what went down in the front yard. No, better not to tell her. A lot of things needed to happen by Monday.

CHAPTER 18

JESSIE

A gentle, soft hand smoothed my hair back.

"Honey, do you want to get up now and eat something?" Grandma hovered over me. "I didn't want to wake you, but I thought you should have some dinner."

"I'm hungry, so I'm glad you woke me." I sat up and rubbed the sleep out of my eyes. "Did everybody else already eat?" I said.

"Yes. Come in the kitchen, and I'll explain while I heat up your dinner," she said.

Explain? That didn't sound good.

Shivering, I put Grandma's soft terrycloth robe on over my clothes and shuffled into the kitchen. I sat down at the table while Grandma put my plate together.

"Where are Mom and Dad?"

"I asked them to go home." She paused for a few minutes. "I found out your dad hit Brian."

I stood up. "Where is he?" Concern for my brother seared through me.

"He's okay. He's asleep on the couch. You two are exhausted, which makes perfect sense in light of what's going on in your lives."

My heart started to slow again. "Did you see Dad hit Brian?"

"No, but I noticed Brian's swollen bottom lip, so I asked him what happened. When he didn't answer right away, I knew," she said.

"Wow, I can't believe this happened and I missed it," I said.

"It didn't go down well with your parents, but that's their problem. I said this to Brian as well: I'm sorry I didn't act sooner." Her eyes started to tear and overflow onto her soft wrinkled cheeks.

I became a hopeless mess as soon as Grandma started to cry. She was a part of so many good memories. She'd bought me every piece of candy I had ever asked for and hid it from Mom. I tended to be hyper, so Mom didn't let me have much candy. It was our little secret. She would also make me absolutely anything to eat, even though she knew I couldn't consume that much food. One morning, I asked for French toast, oatmeal, bacon and hot chocolate. When she put it in front of me, Grandpa looked at her with his brows raised.

"Oh hush," she said as she waved him off.

Grandpa sat at the table, chuckled and shook his head. "You're hungry, huh?" he said, his voice low and smooth.

"Breakfast is the most important meal of the day." I smiled back at him with a mouth full of French toast and syrup smeared across my lips.

I missed Grandpa, with his brown weathered skin and his cool Indian jewelry. You only had to be near him to trust him. Of course, I couldn't finish my breakfast.

"I wanted to tell you at times. I wish I would have," I said as I picked at my nails.

"I will never let him hurt you or Brian again. I will protect you until the last breath leaves my body," she said.

An enormous weight lifted from my shoulders. Finally, an adult I could depend on; someone would save us. I lifted my arms for Grandma to give me a hug. The sobs and tears came in waves. Grandma cried along with me.

"We better stop crying or we won't be able to see with our swollen eyes." We looked at each other and chuckled, our faces already a mess.

"Let me get your dinner and you can eat while we watch a movie. You pick one out," she said.

I picked *About Time*, a film with Rachel McAdams in it. Grandma and I both loved it. I snuggled up to her on the couch and balanced my plate in my lap. I cut into the roasted turkey with relish. I added mashed potato to my fork with a little dip in the gravy. It didn't get any better. I made myself eat some green beans. Without Brian eating my food and Grandma giving me generous portions, I don't think I had eaten as much in a while. *About Time* was no match for the heavy meal. With a full belly, I drifted to sleep in utter contentment.

A few hours later, I awoke on the couch. Grandma had put a quilt over me. I looked over to see Brian on the other couch asleep. I crept over to him, so I could view the condition of his lip. It still looked a little swollen but would look normal in a day or two. As I studied his face, his eyes slowly opened.

"Hey, what're you doing?" he reached his arms over his head to stretch.

"Just checking out the damage to your lip."

"Did Grandma fill you in on Mom and Dad? She sent them packing, it was awesome," he said.

"Yes, she told me. How nuts is that?" I said.

"I don't think anything could get nuttier than you threatening Dad." Brian made a face at me like 'what the hell?' I made the same face right back at him.

"What are you talking about? That's not even funny," I said.

"Uh, you came out of the house after he hit me. You had Grandma's kitchen knife in your hand."

"Are you crazy? I would never," I said.

Brian sat up and stared me in the eye. "Jessie, you did."

All the blood drained from my head and dropped to my feet. The floor rushed upward to meet my collapsing body.

CHAPTER 19

BRIAN

Jessie crumpled to the floor. I got off the couch and knelt beside her. Her dark hair spread around her pale face. I debated dangling spit over her, but figured that wouldn't work in this situation. I lightly patted her checks.

Her eyes popped open with complete focus two seconds later. I fell backward onto my butt. She sat up, looked at me and then scanned the house.

"Are you okay?" I asked.

She stared at me with blank eyes. "Yes, I'm fine."

"You just fainted," I said.

She shrugged her shoulders. "Whatever. I'm fine now."

Her face appeared harder, more lined, and her eyes were black. I searched her face for any reaction, but it was oddly still.

Something was wrong. "Do you want to talk about what you said to Dad?"

"What's there to talk about? He heard me," she said. She got up from the floor.

"I thought you said you didn't remember?" I was confused.

"I remember," she said.

"You're acting really weird."

"What do you want?" She scowled at me.

I had to cut to the chase. "If you pull a knife on Dad again, he'll kill you."

She drew her lips back from her teeth and said, "No. He. Won't."

"Seriously, you're freaking me out." I scooted away from her.

"Don't worry about it. It is what it is. I'm going to bed," she said.

I shook my head in disbelief and ran my hand through my hair. "Talk to me. What's going on?"

I reached out and caught her wrist as she started to walk away. "Tell me what's wrong."

She looked down at my hand on her wrist. "If you touch me again, I may have to hurt you." She shook my hand off.

"Jessie wouldn't like that," she prowled toward the bedroom with the boneless grace of a cat.

I sat in stunned silence. What the hell? My baby sister had just threatened me. And the really scary part was that I believed her. Never mind her face, the words she used were different, the terms were different. She referred to herself in the third person! My sister never said, 'it is what it is'. She would talk to me if I asked her to. My head couldn't wrap around what was happening. This was way more than girl hormonal craziness.

I looked around the room as if the walls contained answers. I took a deep breath. It was two a.m. There was nothing I could do, so I turned on the TV. I lay back down on the couch and pulled the covers up to my chin. The sky glowed pink and gold when I finally closed my eyes.

· · ·

True to her word, Grandma didn't leave us to deal with our father. On Sunday, she drove us back home. Dad had checked himself into rehab the day before.

We all got out of the car and headed into the house. Mom sat at the dining room table.

Mom spat the words. "He's gone. I hope you're happy now."

She was speaking to Grandma, but I thought, *Yep, I'm pretty happy he's gone.*

Defeated, she sat at the table with dirty hair, bloodshot eyes and a puffy face. Apparently, she had cried all night.

Grandma pressed her lips tightly together.

"Kids, why don't you give Mom and me some time to talk." She waved us down the hallway.

Jessie and I walked to our rooms and put our bags down. Three seconds later, we pressed ourselves against the wall in the hallway, inching toward the dining room. No way were we going to miss this conversation. We could hear Grandma as we got closer.

"Is that how you should greet the children? I would hope you would want to comfort them and assure them their lives will get better," Grandma said.

"I'm sorry, Mom, I'm not perfect like you. This is hard for me to handle," Mom said.

"I don't expect you to be perfect, but I do expect you to be a parent to your children and make them your priority," Grandma said.

"They are my priority, but my husband is also very important to me."

"The same husband who hurt your children physically and emotionally is very important to you? If your father mistreated you in any way, I would have been out the door," Grandma said.

Mom's words were broken by sobs, "This is the only man I have ever loved. The only man who has ever truly loved me. It's not that simple. You know his own father abused him and he tries so hard to be a better parent to our children. You have the wrong idea of what is really going on here," Mom said.

"You're kidding yourself. I've talked to the kids. I know I don't have the wrong impression." Grandma exhaled a weary sigh. "The time when you think about what you want is over. The children are your priority."

Mom hiccupped, and her breath came in gasps.

"Pull yourself together," Grandma said, her tone sharp, demanding, like she was talking to child. A minute ticked by. Grandma's voice softened. "I know you can. Why don't you go rest, and I will get the kids settled in? I can stay until they leave for school tomorrow. Is that okay with you?"

"Does it matter if it's okay with me or not? You'll stay if you want to."

Mom's chair scraped against the floor as she pushed back from the table. We hauled ass back to Jessie's room, grabbed a deck of cards and pretended to play. Mom stopped at the doorway a few moments later and leaned against the doorframe. Her blue eyes reflected defeat.

"I'm sorry. I don't know what to say, except I'm sorry," Her eyes moved from me to Jessie.

I watched Jessie to see her reaction, but she lowered her gaze. Without looking at Mom, she asked a question. "Why are you sorry? Are you sorry we were treated badly?" Her eyes flicked upward. "I bet you're not. You're only sorry he's not here, that's it." The words dropped from her lips like a grenade.

Mom said nothing. After a few seconds, she moved on to her room.

"I hate being in this house," Jessie said with her head hanging down.

"I know, me too." I sighed and went to my room.

I laid down on my bed, stretched with my hands over my head and stared at the ceiling. A chill ran through my body. I couldn't pinpoint why, but I was afraid, a bone deep fear for myself and my sister.

CHAPTER 20

JESSIE

I twirled the lock on my locker and thought how nice it was without Dad at home. I wished Mom possessed the guts to ask him to leave permanently. The thirty days of rehab were almost over. While I stood there, Alex came up behind me, and leaned down to place his cheek next to mine.

"Are you ready for track practice today?" he asked.

I grimaced. "Yes, let the torture begin." His cheek pressed against mine.

I dreaded it in a way: the sore muscles the first week, the realization I would have to build up my endurance again. But it was also something I was compelled to do.

Brian was a good athlete: baseball in the spring and summer, football in the fall. I ran fast. Bottom line, I wanted to follow in my brother's footsteps. If he was an athlete, then I would be one as well.

This year, my added incentive would be Alex's presence on the team. At the end of the school day, I headed to the gymnasium and the girl's locker room. I changed into my shorts, sports bra, t-shirt and running shoes. It was wet and cold outside, so we practiced three days a week indoors until March.

I entered the large gymnasium with its polished hardwood floors and white walls. I shivered in my shorts. The boys' team stretched, led by their track coach. The girls still gathered. I sat on the cold hardwood floor but angled myself so that I could still see Alex as well.

I gave him a small wave. He winked backed at me, flashing a casual smile. I loved his easygoing confidence.

Coach Wilson appeared, and the girls headed to the stairwell to start practice.

"All right ladies, I thought we'd start the year with a little fun," he said. "I want you to separate into two teams. You'll race against your own teammates today."

Rebecca queued up behind me in line. I turned to her and said, "There is no way I am letting one of these girls beat me."

"I know what you mean, but we're the youngest this year. I don't know if we will keep our spots on the relay teams." She chewed on her thumbnail.

"If I sit out the relays, I'm going to be pissed." I liked racing; it suited my competitive nature.

I queued up to race in the next lap. Of course, Amanda was beside me. Before I could roll my eyes, the whistle sounded, and we rushed forward.

I built up so much speed hurtling through the narrow hallway that I almost crashed into the wall trying to make the turn. We basically ran in a large square, our running shoes squeaking furiously against the tile floors. My rapid breathing echoed off the lockers. Amanda remained two steps behind me at most. No way was this bitch beating me. I careened around the corner and tried to maintain my speed. In my peripheral vision, I could see her hesitate on the last turn. I cut her off and took a definitive lead as we finished. Yes!

A minute later, I turned to her and said, "Nice run," my lips twisted in a smart-ass smile. Rebecca, waiting her turn, gave me a low-five as

I passed by. After the races, we jogged up and down the steps for conditioning. Rebecca ran in front of me this time.

"I'm going to die," I panted as we continued to jog up the steps.

"Shut up, or I'll barf on you."

"I'll shut up, but why do we run track?" It must be temporary insanity, I decided, because practice sucked on so many levels.

To my amazement, my rubbery legs continued to lift me to the next step. Twenty-five excruciating minutes later, practice wound down and the team headed back to the locker rooms.

My legs wobbled as we walked through the school lobby. Someone opened the front doors and a cold, wet wind blew into the school. Some of the boys from the track team stood in the lobby talking.

"Hey, how was practice?" one of them called to us.

"Brutal. How about you guys?"

As we chatted in the vestibule, I started to shake from the cold wind circling my bare legs and sweat-dampened skin. Will, a sophomore on the team—who also happened to be gorgeous in a blond, Greek god kind of way—stood beside me.

"Do you want my jacket? I'm not cold." He took off his jacket and held it out to me. I hesitated, until another big gust of wind blew up my shorts, changing my mind.

"Thanks, it's freezing in here." I swung his jacket around my shoulders and relished in the warmth, noticing the light linen cologne smell that clung to it. Will had the long and lanky build of a runner. I smiled my thanks. My eyes drifted to the floor. My go-to gesture when feeling awkward.

When I lifted my eyes, I noticed Alex marching toward us with an annoyed expression.

"Wow, its cold in here. I wonder why they have the doors propped open." He stared at Will's jacket and then possessively draped his arm around my shoulder.

"They're delivering some equipment," Will responded.

"Yeah, probably. Thanks for lending her your jacket." Alex looked Will directly in the eyes, then swiped the jacket from my shoulders and thrust it back at him.

Will met Alex's glare. A non-verbal challenge had been issued, it seemed, and based on Will's steady return gaze, it was *challenge accepted*.

Seriously? He might as well just have peed on me to mark his territory. I could feel the blood rushing to my cheeks as Will took his jacket. I exchanged a quick look of *can you believe this shit* with Rebecca.

Rebecca shook her head.

"I've got to change, talk to you guys later," I said.

Alex strode away from the group to catch up with me. He asked in a lowered voice, "Was Will hitting on you?"

"No," I said, exasperated. "He was just being polite. I was shaking from the cold."

"I doubt it. I've seen him checking you out," Alex said.

"The girl still has to be interested in him for it to go somewhere, and I'm only interested in you," I said as I squeezed his hand.

He leaned into me and gave me a long kiss, a kiss that conveyed his possessiveness just in case Will watched.

"See you tomorrow." He playfully smacked my butt as he turned away. I hated when he did that; it was so demeaning. As he disappeared around the corner, I noticed my track coach in the gymnasium doorway; he had witnessed the whole exchange. I was ridiculously embarrassed. *Again.*

Coach Wilson walked over to me. "You know, I just don't like that kid with you," he said.

His comment surprised me. "Why would you say that?"

"He has some things on his mind that you don't. You're a great girl, and I don't want to see you go down the wrong path because of a guy."

"That's never going to happen. I'm smarter than that," I said. My stubborn streak kicked in.

"All right." He raised his hands in surrender. "I'm just watching out for you." He chuckled. "But hey, I know your brother will keep an eye on you."

"Perfect. Alex loves that," I said sarcastically. "He already feels like he has to be careful because of Brian."

"Well, that's a good thing." Coach Wilson gave me a half smile and strolled back into the gym.

What did Coach Wilson see in Alex that I didn't?

CHAPTER 21

BRIAN

I quickly showered and toweled off in the locker room since I needed to drive Jessie and Rebecca home. Alex joked around with his buddies near the row of lockers in the back. I could hear his big mouth.

"I already told you: she's down for it. It's going to happen for sure," he said.

Fire ran up my back. I silently moved behind him. He whipped around.

"You better not be talking about my sister, ass-wipe." I stood close to him, keeping my eyes locked on his. Nothing like a little intimidation to make my point.

"No, hey man, just joking around. I wasn't talking about Jessie," he said, his eyes wide.

"You better not be." I flipped my hand at his buddies like they were annoying flies. "The rest of you get out of here. I don't want to look at you." His friends scrambled.

"I need to speak to you alone. Wait right here." I finished getting dressed. It was good to be the king. Alex turned the other way to wait for me.

"Alex," I said. He turned around to look at me. I was an inch or two taller than him and more muscled. "That crap you just said; it better not be about my sister." I paused to let it sink in. "You keep your pants zipped up, because if I hear anything different, I will significantly hurt you," I said.

He was silent for a minute. He nodded his head and left the locker room without saying a word.

The punk. If he did touch my sister, he would get the ass beating of a lifetime. I didn't even want to consider Jessie going through the ordeal Tracey and I just endured. The mere thought of Alex messing with my sister made me insane.

I shut my locker as Will passed by me.

"I'm so glad you said something to him. He's always talking smack. I hate that kid."

"Yeah, I'm not a fan either." I planned to tell Jessie about Alex's comment.

CHAPTER 22

JESSIE

Tight jeans: check.

Cell phone: check.

Smokey eye makeup: check.

Ready to go, Ally, Kristi and I loaded into Brian's car. A new eighteen-and-under dance club had just opened, and Tracey wanted to go, so Brian offered to take us.

"Thanks for the ride," Ally said as soon as we got into the backseat. I mouthed to her, "Suck-up." She stuck her tongue out at me.

I sat forward and put my arms around Tracey's shoulders in the front seat. "I'm so excited! Hanging out in Burger King is beyond boring."

She patted my arms and gave them a squeeze. "I know, me too. Good thing your big bro is willing to tough it out with me." She grinned at him.

Brian winked at her. The apparent love on his face every time he looked at her made me happy.

"Thanks for taking us, Brian," I said, to echo Ally.

"You are welcome, ladies. I'm expecting my martyr status any day from the Pope for putting up with all of you," he said.

"Oh, shut up!" I rolled my eyes at him and settled into the backseat. For the rest of the ride, we did what we always did in the car together.

We sang every song that came on the radio. We must not have sounded too bad, as Brian didn't comment or turn the station.

We arrived at the club; the parking lot was packed. The rest of the high school was excited about something new to do. We lived in the suburbs of Middle of Nowhere, Ohio. We were easily entertained.

We all piled into the club and went straight to the dance floor. I couldn't wait.

"I don't know how you do it," I said to Kristi, as I watched her roll her hips.

"You can do it; you just need to loosen up and relax," she said.

"I don't think my hips get that loose," I said.

We laughed. It was so fun to dance. I scanned the crowd every few minutes looking for Alex.

Tracey tried to get Brian out on the dance floor, but he wouldn't budge.

"Hey, sweetie," Alex said, as he snuck up behind me.

"Hey, you made it."

I kissed him, then leaned back away from him, "You smell like beer." I searched his face for signs of drunkenness. His eyes were clear, but a little bloodshot.

"No biggie, we drank a couple on the way here," he said.

He didn't look drunk, but I despised the smell of beer. "Can we talk over here for a minute?"

"Sure," he said.

I took his hand and led him off the dance floor into one of the booths. "You've been drinking?" I said.

"That's what I said." He gave me a lopsided grin. "Topher and the guys picked me up and they had a twelve pack. We drank a few. I'm not drunk or anything." He studied my face uncertainly.

"Okay." I looked down at my feet and crossed my arms over my chest while I struggled to accept this as no big deal. It wasn't a big deal for a lot of kids, but it was a big deal with me. It made me feel like a baby. I couldn't bear to be reminded about my sucky home life or my father when I was with my friends.

Alex waited for me to continue.

I took a deep breath and blurted my concern. "My dad drinks a lot. He has for as long as I can remember." My voice wavered. "Anyway, he's very mean and drinking makes him worse. I can't remember which came first, the drunkenness or the meanness."

He pulled me into an embrace. "I'm sorry, why haven't you told me before?"

"It's not something I like to talk about. I'm sure you can imagine why," I said.

"I get it. I wouldn't want to talk about it either," he said.

The concern and care were obvious on his face. I would love him forever.

"Even the smell of beer gives me bad vibes. I would really like it if my boyfriend didn't smell like beer." I smiled awkwardly at him.

He reached into his jacket pocket, pulled out some gum, and popped a piece in his mouth. "Issue solved. Now my breath is minty fresh. Do you want to kiss me and check?"

I stared into his eyes and prayed he understood the seriousness of this issue. Hesitantly, I leaned over and placed my lips on his. He gripped my lower back and pulled me closer.

After a few minutes, he broke away, but kept his forehead on mine. "This is what I love about you. No drama, you just state the problem and move on."

"So, are we okay on the beer thing?" I asked.

"Yes, I don't care about beer," he said. He kissed me again and time seemed to slip away.

Kristi pulled me from my kissy haze by yelling from the dance floor, "Jessie, our favorite song! Get out here."

"I Can't Feel My Face" thumped out of the speakers. I kept Alex's hand in mine and joined my friends.

"Oh no, I'm not dancing," Alex said, as he backed away. "You girls have fun. I'll be over by Topher."

"This song reminds me of us, you have to dance. I smile at you so much my cheeks go numb," I said.

He laughed. "You're so cute, but no way on dancing, sorry."

"Aww, come on, be brave," I said, but he kept waving his hands in the "no way is this happening" gesture. I made a sad face at him, but that didn't work either.

"I can't feel my face when I'm with you," Kristi and I sang to each other. "Yes, I know."

The DJ started to mix the song, "Talk Too Much" in and all three of us screamed.

"You know I talk too much, honey come put your lips on mine and shut me up!" We screamed the lyrics to each other on the dance floor with complete abandon.

Out of the corner of my eye, I noticed Will on the dance floor; he obviously wasn't afraid to dance. I loved people who weren't afraid to put it out there and have fun. He was smart too, as he had plenty of girls to dance with him.

He worked his way through the crowd toward us. Kristi, the only single girl in our group, was more than happy to dance with him.

The dance floor was so crowded with people, I could no longer see the booths surrounding it. The lights pulsed red, pink and blue in time with the music. The girls and I danced, but we were fairly smashed together. A heavy weight crashed into my back. My knees bent to hold the weight and my hands shot out to break the fall. Someone grabbed my extended arm and pulled me to the side. Arms wrapped around me. I looked up; Will held me. I turned around to see what had fallen on me: a big guy lay on the floor laughing.

He got up and leaned into my face, so I could hear him. "I'm so sorry. My friends and I were pushing each other. We're assholes." He appeared genuinely sorry. I smelled beer on his breath. Obviously, some students had been drinking before they arrived at the club.

"I'm okay, it's no problem." I waved him away, so he would stop apologizing.

"Are you okay?" Will asked.

I could hardly hear him over the music, but I could read his lips. I got up on my tiptoes to get close enough, so he could hear me. This must be why it's so loud in clubs, I thought. You have to whisper in the other person's ear to be heard. Very intimate.

"Yes, nice save. Thank you," I said.

A slow song started, and Will tightened his arms around me. We swayed to the music. My eyes locked with his and *bam!* An electric shock vibrated through my body. With his hand on my lower back, he pulled my body to his, his lean stomach pressed against me. I couldn't deny our chemistry. It felt right to be in his arms.

"Are you kidding me?" Alex snarled as he gripped Will's shoulder. Will grabbed Alex's hand and threw it off.

I put my body between them. "He just helped me out. This guy knocked me down. That's it. Nothing is going on," I pleaded. He lunged for Will again.

"Bullshit. It didn't look like he was just helping you up."

"Don't get pissed at her," Will said. He moved in front of me. "Craig, hey man, come here." The slow song continued in the background, but we were the main attraction on the dance floor.

The big, drunk guy shuffled over to us.

"Craig, tell Alex you knocked Jessie down."

"Uh, yeah. An accident, but I did knock her down," Craig said.

Alex calmed down, but still looked mad. "Okay, whatever. It looked like more than that to me." He rubbed the back of this neck. "I need to get out of here."

He made his way through the crowd. Topher looked at Ally, shrugged and followed him.

"Alex!" I caught up to him and grabbed his arm. "Don't go. I don't want you to be mad at me. There's nothing going on," I said.

His eyes, desperately sad, stared at me. "Fine Jessie, whatever, but I still want to go."

Ally and Kristi stood on either side of me. A sob escaped my lips. They hustled me over to a booth. The thought of Alex breaking up with me became a real possibility. A possibility so painful it surprised me.

"It's fine. He's upset now, but he'll get over it. He'll realize you weren't doing anything," said Kristi. Ally nodded.

"The thing is, I did hold on to Will." The admission made me cry even more.

"Shit, well, you and Will are the only ones who know that. Alex doesn't. We know it now too, but we aren't telling anyone," Kristi said.

"Exactly," Ally said.

"What's wrong with me? I love Alex. Why would I like Will too?" I asked.

"Cause that's what we do. You're going to like more than one boy. Come on, cut yourself a break. It's harmless flirting," Kristi said.

"Okay." I sniffed and wiped my face on my sleeve.

I asked Kristi to go get my brother, so we could leave. She got up to use the bathroom. Will came up to me while I was sitting in the booth alone.

"Are you okay?"

"Yes, I'm fine. I'm sorry Alex acted like a territorial dog."

"It's not your fault." He reached across the table and squeezed my hand. "I just wanted to make sure you were okay." Our eyes met, and

I could sense the things we weren't saying. He knocked on the table three times before he walked away.

The lights flipped on and I blinked to adjust my eyes. Without the rose glow from the lights, the club appeared dingy and small. I spotted my brother near the entrance. Tracey leaned against him with her head on his shoulder. She looked tired, but I could see the contentment on their faces. They were perfectly at peace with each other. My handsome brother and the girl he loved. Brian was talking to Tim, but he still had his arm around Tracey. He noticed me looking at him and mouthed 'Let's go.'

Ally, Kristi and I followed him to the car and climbed in back. He obviously hadn't heard about the fight with Alex, thank God, or he would have mentioned it. He turned on the radio as we drove away; Tracey and Ally were already falling asleep. I stared out the window and watched the dark landscape roll by. Kristi bumped her shoulder into mine.

"Stop worrying. You worry too much." She gave me a reassuring smile.

"Yeah." I leaned my head on her shoulder and closed my eyes, my mind whirling. I didn't know how to make up with Alex. I guessed I would have to wait for him to cool off. There were too many things on my mind: Alex showing up with beer on his breath, my attraction to Will and a deep uneasiness about my future with Alex.

CHAPTER 23

JESSIE

True to her nature, Mom accepted Dad back from rehab with open arms. True to my nature, I kept my arms crossed tight against my chest and brooded in my room, waiting for them to get home. I paced the small space and acknowledged that neither acceptance nor forgiveness were in my heart. I doubted he'd changed. Any emotional connection to my father had been severed permanently; no apologies or time would repair it. I didn't share Mom's knack for pretending everything was fine.

Dad had written a letter to me while in rehab. Brian and I refused to attend any of the counseling sessions. There was no way in hell I would sit in a room with my him and discuss "issues." The only issue was him.

I read the letter while standing at my bedroom window with the afternoon sunlight highlighting the black-penned words. He apologized and vowed to treat us well, which meant nothing to me. He explained how his father had abused him, which drove his desire to drink. He explained that he didn't remember what happened when he was drunk. It was a complete blank. *Oh, to be so lucky.* He went on to say how hurt he was by his own childhood, the unfairness of it. It was utter bullshit. He excused himself for everything. How convenient for him. I sneered as I read it. He had been treated poorly but had gone on to do the same to his children. I raised my eyes to the ceiling of my bedroom. How could all this hate fit into my body? The letter made me hate him more, if that were even possible. The big kicker, he hoped I would forgive him. Good luck with that, buddy. The odds were nonexistent.

Mom forced us to attend one AA meeting. I sat there and listened to these people and grew furious. I wanted to stand up and shout, '*Oh poor little me.*' A disease excused all their behavior? Wow, I hoped for a disease I could blame all my shit on.

In the real world, these people were terminally selfish and self-absorbed. Screw this whole disease thing.

I heard Mom's car pull into the garage. Oh goody, they were home. Brian and I waited in the kitchen to greet Dad.

"You ready to see asshole?" I asked.

"Nope. You?"

"Never."

From the door, Mom called out, "Daddy's home."

Dad came in behind her and at least had the decency to look uncomfortable. He knew we weren't happy to see him.

"It's so good to see you," he said as he approached me with open arms.

I allowed myself to be hugged but kept my arms at my side. It was completely foreign to be hugged by my father and it made me jittery.

He hugged Brian next. Brian at least put his arms around my father somewhat. He had grown so much bigger than Dad, who, with his gray hair and smaller stature, was showing his age.

Dad heartily patted him on the back and said, "You've grown in a month. Mom, can you believe how big our boy has gotten?"

They exchanged looks of mutual congratulation, and I could see the pride in Dad's eyes as he looked at Brian. He never gazed adoringly at me this way. It didn't make me jealous, just curious about why I was left out.

"Kids, let's sit down in the living room for a minute," Dad said.

Brian and I sat on the beige love seat together while Mom and Dad sat on the matching couch. I picked at the weave of the fabric. I didn't want to have a chat with either of them.

"I just wanted to tell you how sorry I am about how I've treated you. When I'm drunk, I become someone I don't like or recognize. I don't remember much of the things I've done. I only know what Mom told me. It will be better now. I have learned how to deal with my illness," he said.

Mom told him what he had done? I almost laughed. Bet it was the *'crazy light'* version of his behavior.

"I'm going to attend your sporting events and try to have more of a relationship with you both," he said. He took a deep breath and let it out slowly. Mom put her arm around him.

I heroically squelched the desire to roll my eyes.

He cleared his throat and said, "How does that sound to you two?"

Brian spoke first. "It sounds good." He always was more agreeable than me. I liked to hold a good grudge.

"What do you think?" Dad raised his eyes to me expectantly.

Before I could even consider my response, I said, "Some things can't be fixed. Words can't be unsaid. Actions can't be undone."

Brian and Mom gasped. I maintained eye contact with difficulty. My eyes showed my emotion and right now that emotion was disgust. He would have to do a lot to make up our childhood to us, but at the end of the day, I didn't want to have a relationship with him, whether he'd changed or not.

"That's a fair response. I deserve your anger, but I would like to try and make it up to you."

Mom looked me with a pained expression. She could kiss my ass. I didn't like her a whole lot, either.

"I don't want to talk right now. Excuse me." I rose from the couch. Brian gave me a sideways glance, but I stomped back to my room. I put my headphones in and plopped down on my bed. I would no longer pretend everything was fine.

CHAPTER 24

JESSIE

Relief flooded through my body as Monday dawned. I couldn't stand another minute in our fake happy, chatty home. It happened to be my birthday as well. The big fifteen. I bit my bottom lip and wondered how my day would go with Alex. We'd talked on the phone and texted, but I didn't think he'd forgiven me for the dance with Will. I wasn't over the dance with Will either.

Brian knocked on my open bedroom door. "Since I'm a saint, I'll give you and Rebecca a ride to school today."

"Cool, thanks." I texted Rebecca, grabbed my bag and followed him out the door.

He picked up Tracey as usual, and we arrived at school with time to spare. As we unloaded from the car, Tracey pulled a card out of her bag.

"Happy Birthday!" She smiled as she handed it to me.

"Oh yeah." Brian dug in his front jean pocket and pulled something out. He offered the crumpled object, wrapped in tissue paper.

I took it from his hand and unwrapped it. Inside was a leather bracelet with a quarter-sized, silver symbol attached in the middle. The symbol was a circle, with five spokes.

Warmth spread through my chest. "It's so cool, thank you," I said.

"The symbol means seeking balance. It's Hindu. I made it in shop class," Brian said.

Only Brian and I knew how important it was for me to seek balance. "So cool," I said again, grinning. Tracey tied the bracelet around my wrist.

"He made me one too," she said as she extended her wrist to show me.

I gave Tracey a hug, but Brian backed away from me.

"Don't hug me in public, it's embarrassing," he said as he held his hands up. I slapped his arm instead.

"Remember we have dinner tonight. We'll pick you up around six-thirty," I said to Rebecca as we parted ways.

Alex, Kristi and Ally were standing next to my locker, which had a couple of pink and white balloons taped to it.

"Happy Birthday," they said in chorus. Alex gave me a hug and handed me a birthday card.

I grimaced at all of them as I opened it…a second later the card erupted with loud singing, "They say it's your birthday! We're gonna have a good time!" I quickly snapped the card shut. "Okay, you're killing me. I guess you're going for embarrassment?" I gave all three of them my squinty-eyed look.

"Oh, come on, it's fun," Ally said.

"For you, maybe." I gave them both a hug. I turned to Alex as I opened my locker. He leaned against the adjoining locker in all his perfect guy-gorgeousness.

"I have your gift, but I'll give it to you before track practice," he said.

"Are we okay?" I said. Sadness lingered in his eyes.

"Yeah, I guess. It bothered me to see you with another guy. It made me feel crazy," he said. He tugged at my belt loop.

"I only want to be with you." I reached over and laid my hand against his cheek.

He only nodded, but as we walked down the hall, our fingers laced together, I hoped this meant we were on good terms again.

I breezed into the office for my free period, feeling lightheaded with relief. I sat down and doodled *Alex Corbin* on the inside of my math folder.

"Jessie?" Mrs. Palmer's voice snapped me back to reality.

I went into her office. "Hi, Mrs. Palmer. Did you want to talk to me?"

"Yes. I'm sorry it's been weeks since we last talked. I've been booked with other students. As the only counselor, my schedule is a nightmare."

"It's okay," I said.

"Come in. How were the holidays?" She studied me expectantly.

"Great. Alex gave me this necklace." I proudly lifted the gold chain so she could see the small heart locket.

"How nice. I may need to have Alex give my husband some tips," she chuckled.

I made a that-must-suck face to convey my sympathy.

"Oh, it's not that bad," she said and laughed again.

She checked my file while I fidgeted in the chair. I wished I'd kept my concerns to myself.

"How did it go at home over the holiday break?"

"It was fine," I said quietly.

"Anymore dissociative episodes?"

I took in a deep breath and slowly let it out. "I don't want to talk about it anymore. I'm sorry, I know you're trying to help me, but I'm fine."

Instead of conveying my okay-ness, I started to cry. Mrs. Palmer gently handed me some tissues.

"You don't seem fine. Tell me what's wrong," she said.

Words tumbled from my mouth before I could stop them. "There was another fight between my dad and brother. The fight was so bad, my grandma forced Dad to check himself into rehab."

Tears streamed down my face, no doubt causing my mascara to smear along with them.

"The worst part is I don't remember the fight. I remember arriving at Grandma's and then waking up from a nap. Nothing in between… and that's when the fight happened. Brian said I broke up their fight and shouted at Dad."

I decided not to mention his revelation that I'd pulled a knife on Dad. God only knows what would happen then.

"Now my Dad is back from rehab; I hate it and I hate him. I liked life a lot better without him in it," I said.

"I'm sorry. I can't imagine how hard this is for you." She paused for a moment and then asked, "Did you attend any of the sessions with your dad during rehab?"

"No, why?" I asked.

"They may have discussed coping skills you could use once your dad returned home," she said.

"Mom tried to make us go, but Brian would miss conditioning practice and there was no way I was going if Brian wasn't."

"Okay. Your parents haven't returned my calls, so I'm going to reach out another way. You need to talk about these dissociative episodes with a doctor and discuss ways to manage your stress. It's time to get serious," she said.

My stomach contents surged up my throat. I swallowed hard.

"Please don't do that. It will only make things worse," I begged. "My Dad will go nuts if he thinks I'm telling you about his behavior."

"You need help and maybe your parents should wake up and realize what they're doing to you," she said.

"Can't you help me?" my voice cracked.

She stretched her hand toward me across her desk. "I wish I could, but I'm not a doctor and you need to talk with someone who is more familiar with what you're experiencing."

My hand covered my mouth. "Mrs. Palmer, can I be excused? I feel sick." God knew what information I would blurt out next.

"Okay." She frowned.

I fled from the office to the bathroom and into a stall. I leaned my head against the cool metal of the door. What the hell was I doing? I stood there for a few minutes until my heart slowed. I spit into the toilet. Finally, I opened the door and went over to the sink and splashed cold water on my face. My hands shook. I looked into the mirror to wipe the mascara from under my eyes. My hand hesitated in midair. Confusion clouded my brain. Who was this girl?

"Hey Jess." A girl from biology class greeted me as she entered the bathroom.

"Hey." I lifted one side of my mouth to smile. My gazed flicked back to the mirror. The girl in the mirror could take my place. I could disappear, turn inward and never return. Some part of me knew this option existed. Right then, I desperately wanted oblivion.

The image in the mirror scared me. The bell for my next class rang, triggering my mind back into my body.

I left the bathroom and stumbled to biology class. Normally, biology held my interest, but not today. I stared out the window, seeing nothing until a flash of red caught my attention. A male cardinal sat perched on a tree branch. Cardinals were my favorite bird. I knew he was a male based on his bright red color. Females were more of a brownish-red. He sat on the branch and stared right at me. I had read a book on omens and the spiritual meaning associated with seeing certain birds. Cardinals represented your deceased loved ones paying you a visit. Maybe it was Grandpa. *Grandpa, if that's you, help me in whatever way you can.* The cardinal sat on the branch watching me for the rest of class.

The school day blurred by after my counseling drama. Before I knew it, I was back at my locker getting my track bag for practice. I needed to talk to Brian.

I sensed him before I felt him. Alex came up behind me and put his cheek next to mine. His smell and the warmth of his skin against mine soothed me. He held a beautifully wrapped, blue package in his hand.

I gazed up at him as I unwrapped the present. Perfume. I took a tentative sniff and was pleasantly surprised. "I love it. It smells perfect. You're so sweet," I said.

"I know smell is a big deal for you, so I wanted to pick a special perfume. Something I knew you would like."

"Thank you." I reached up to hug him. I was so flattered he'd taken the time to select the right gift. Being important to him only fanned my love. He wrapped his arms around me and picked me up to whisper in my ear.

"Happy Birthday. I love you," he said.

I gazed into his blue eyes and said, "I love you too." I snuggled my head under his neck and breathed in his smell. The smell I related to love and comfort. He rested his head on top of mine and kept his arms around me. We stood embracing each other for several minutes.

"I hate to leave you, but I've got to run down to the gym to catch Brian. I have to remind him that Rebecca and I need a ride home." Reluctantly, I dropped my arms from his waist.

"Okay, I'll see you at practice," he said.

I gave him a quick kiss, shouldered my bag and ran down the hallway toward the gym.

The halls were empty as I ran down them and the steps to reach the gym. I didn't see Brian in there, so I went around the corner to the boy's locker room.

A couple of guys were getting ready to walk in when I called out to them, "Hey, could you send Brian Taylor out if he's in there?" I asked.

"Sure." They went inside and I heard one of them yell, "Hey Brian, there's a hot girl outside the locker room who wants to talk to you."

Idiots. My cheeks burned. I leaned against the painted cement wall and waited for him. The door opened and he peeked out.

He yelled back, "It's my sister, you morons."

"What's wrong?" he said. I wasn't in the habit of chasing him down.

"Long story short, I talked with Mrs. Palmer and I've said too much and now she wants Mom and Dad to come in and discuss my issues." I rubbed my forehead.

Brian scrutinized my face. "We agreed you wouldn't talk to her again."

"I don't know, she asks me how I'm doing. I answer her questions." I shrugged.

Guys walked by and cast sidelong glances at us on the way to the locker room.

"We can't talk here," Brian said. "Let's talk tonight when we get home. Calm down, we'll figure something out."

"Okay," I mumbled. I wasn't brave enough to tell him about the girl in the bathroom mirror. The one who wanted to disappear.

CHAPTER 25

BRIAN

I slammed the car door and revved the cherry mufflers to life with their smooth purr. As we drove home, I considered Jessie's problem. Jessie talking to the counselor bothered me and her crazy behavior worried me. One minute, goofy and sweet; the next, cold and calculated. Now the school counselor wanted Mom and Dad to come in and talk to her. What a nightmare. Dad would kill Jessie for telling a counselor our family problems. That couldn't happen.

The sun made its final descent as I pulled into our driveway. Jessie had been quiet the whole way home. "Hey, let's talk before we go in."

Jessie nodded.

"You have to avoid the counselor, I hate to think what you'll say next. You haven't been yourself lately," I said.

"I know." She kept picking at her fingernails. "I'm scared." She paused and then said in starts and stops, "Sometimes, I feel like I don't know myself…I don't remember threatening Dad…I'm losing it. I can't hold myself together." She pressed her hands to the side of her head. Her eyes stared forward, wide-opened and afraid.

"We talked about it at Grandma's house," he insisted. "Remember? In the middle of the night."

"No, that's what I'm telling you. I don't remember most of our visit to Grandma's." She sobbed and hiccupped.

"Don't cry." I lightly pushed her shoulder. "Mom will think I tortured you on your birthday."

Jessie wiped her tears. I said the next words as if I could force my will into her.

"You'll keep it together. It's just stress. You're strong and you can do this. I'll help you through it, but from now on, this is our secret. Don't tell anyone else."

She nodded again.

"Mrs. Palmer mentioned this thing called dissociative disorder a few times."

"I don't want you to worry about it." I waited till her eyes met mine. "I'll figure it out. Okay?"

"Okay, but will you check into it?" she asked.

"Yeah."

I could see the trust in her face. We hadn't been like normal siblings. We were soldiers bonded in battle, leave no man behind. We hadn't fought or competed for our parent's attention. We survived.

"Come on, let's go. They're going to wonder why we're sitting in the driveway," I said.

As soon as she opened the kitchen door, Mom and Dad shouted, "Happy Birthday!" Mom hugged Jessie first, then Dad. When Dad hugged Jessie, her arms just hung at her sides. I wondered if he noticed.

"Are you hungry for your steak dinner, sweetie?" Mom asked. Since Dad had come home, Mom had been working overtime to play out her happy family routine.

"Yeah, I'm hungry, we just need to stop and pick up Rebecca."

Like all the good restaurants, the local steakhouse was downtown. It was decorated in an Old West theme, with a deep porch and rocking chairs. A great place to people watch in the summer. If you went out in Stanton, downtown was the only place to go. We pulled into the parking lot and got out. The scent of fresh steak wafting through the parking lot made my mouth water.

"Smells good, doesn't it, buddy?" Dad clapped me on the back. He beamed and his hand lingered on my shoulder a moment. My muscles tensed under his hand.

"Absolutely." I pressed my lips in a grimace.

The restaurant glowed with dimly lit candles and lanterns. The floors were wide, maple-stained, dusty-looking planks. Our table, near the back of the restaurant, was a large rounded booth with padded red leather seats. As soon as we sat down, our server brought over a wicker basket of warm fresh bread with butter. I couldn't wait to stuff my face.

"Miss, do you mind bringing two more baskets of bread? He'll be done with this one in two minutes." Mom smiled at her.

"Of course." The waitress winked at me.

Forget the 'eat less red meat' movement, we all ordered steak. I ordered an eight-ounce filet mignon and Jessie the smaller six-ounce filet. Dinner would cost Dad a pretty penny.

As the waitress cleared our salad plates, another server brought our steaks. I could hardly wait for everyone to get their plates. Finally, I cut my first piece and put it in my mouth. The juicy and perfectly seasoned steak melted on my tongue.

"Oh man, this is amazing." I couldn't hold back a food moan.

"It's awesome." Jessie looked at me, her eyes bright. "This is one dinner I'm not sharing with you."

"I bet." I winked at her and then turned to Dad. "Thanks, Dad, for dinner."

"You're welcome. It's our pleasure." He picked up his glass of iced tea. "Mom and I would like to give a toast to Jessie. Happy Birthday, sweetheart."

Jessie said thank you. She mostly looked at her plate or talked quietly with Rebecca. Thank God for Rebecca; she made dinner bearable.

Our group was quiet for a birthday party. At the end of the meal, they brought out a chocolate birthday cake with fifteen candles. It was always chocolate cake for Jessie.

Just to get her worked up I said, "Let's call the waitress over so we can all sing happy birthday."

She shook her head vigorously. "No, let's not sing happy birthday so I don't die."

I laughed. "Calm down, I'm just messing with you."

Rebecca elbowed my side. She mouthed, "LAME." I just chuckled.

I studied Jessie's face, lit up by the candles. The purple circles under her eyes made her look tired. Our family life had taken its toll. Jessie and Rebecca cut big pieces of cake for themselves. They looked alike: dark hair, about the same height, and a similar build. Rebecca handed me a piece of cake. As I dug in, I thought it was good that Jessie had a friend like her.

For once, my stomach felt full after dinner. The second piece of chocolate cake put me over the edge. As we made our way out, we noticed our neighbors, Ted and Alyssa, hosting a party in a secluded private dining room. They insistently waved us over.

I liked them. They let us swim in their pool all the time and would sit down and talk to us. They didn't have children of their own, but were always great with Jessie and me.

Mom and Dad said hello as we stood behind them, and I took in the room while they chatted. Carnival-themed decorations dominated the room. Silver and gold streamers hung from the ceiling. The waitresses wore long flowy black skirts and white blouses. When my parents started talking to our other neighbors, Alyssa tapped my arm.

"Hey, it's good to see you. You guys should check out the fortune teller. She's really good." She said in a lower voice, "Ted paid a fortune for her, so please get a reading."

I looked in the direction she'd indicated. Dressed in black with a heavy shawl over her shoulders, the woman sat in a booth alone. Her black hair showed streaks of grey. She was staring at Jessie. While I watched, she motioned for Jessie to come to her.

"I forgot your and Jessie's birthdays were so close. Happy birthday," I said.

"Thank you. Your mom told us you would be here celebrating Jessie's birthday, so she said you all would stop by. I'm glad we got to see you. Ted is going all out for my fortieth. Half of the neighborhood is in this room," she laughed.

"I see that." I smiled back at her, but my eyes were drawn toward the older woman. She held Jessie's palm and leaned across the table to speak to her. The corners of Jessie's mouth turned down and her jaw clenched.

"I'll check out the fortune teller. Looks like she's reading Jessie's palm."

Alyssa glanced over at them. "Oh good. Yes, definitely have her read your palm."

As I approached Jessie from behind, I heard her say, "My birthday is today."

The woman's eyes met mine briefly.

"No, today is not your birthday. Forgive me for sharing this information, but you must know. You need to hear what I have to tell you. You are a Gemini, the sign of the Twins, born at the end of May. One twin is from the light; the other is dark," she said.

"No, that's not right. My birthday is today." She pulled her hand back and started to get up, but the woman grabbed her wrist.

"Please, you must listen. I'm sorry, but I have to say what I can. I must tell you. Today is not your birthday. I've never seen anyone so shadowed...no, dominated by their sign. The twins rule your life. You must choose your light nature. If you allow your dark nature—your dark twin—she'll take over, the light twin will be lost," she said.

"Stop, you're scaring her." I shoved myself into the booth beside my sister.

"Again, I am sorry. Here, please take my card." She reached out and pushed her card into my hand. An electric current joined our hands. "Keep my card. You will need to contact me."

I glanced at the card, "Natalia Moretti, Psychic Medium." It had her phone number as well.

She squeezed my hand. "She knows you as her brother in this life, and that is good. She needs you. Your voice will be the only one she hears."

"Why are you saying all this shit?" My anger built as Jessie trembled beside me.

"Some things must be said, regardless of time or place." Natalia's eyes darted toward our approaching parents. She reached for Jessie's hand again. "She has shown up already, hasn't she?" she stared at Jessie's face and then continued. "The dark twin inside of you is powerful; don't give in to her."

The palm reader rose quickly from the booth, uttered a few foreign words and flicked her fingers toward our parents. Her hand motion and the way she spat the words indicated something bad, maybe a curse. She turned and went the opposite direction. I watched her exit the room like a ghost. One minute there, the next gone.

"You guys ready to go?" Mom examined us expectantly.

"We're ready." I bumped Jessie and put my hand under her elbow to pull her out of the booth. I lowered my head close to hers. "Ignore her. She's nuts. She tried to scare you, that's all."

She didn't answer but kept her eyes downcast. She shuffled beside me as we left the room. Rebecca bounced over to us.

"Ted and Alyssa are so cool. Awesome party." She nudged Jessie.

"Did you see the cute waiter I talked too?"

"No, I talked to the fortune teller," Jessie said in a lifeless tone.

"Too much cake, right Jess?" I said.

"Yes. Too much cake," she said.

"Ugh, that sucks." Rebecca said.

The three of us squeezed into the backseat for the ride home. Jessie put her head on Rebecca's shoulder and closed her eyes. I stared out the car window into the darkness and tried to shake off what the gypsy had said. It scared the shit out of me because it felt true.

As soon as we got home, I went into my room to look up the disorder Jessie had mentioned earlier. WebDoc's listing popped up:

Dissociative Identity Disorder

Dissociative identity disorder is difficult to diagnose and harder to treat, but research findings suggest it's a psychological response to personal and family-related stress, especially during early childhood when emotional neglect or abuse may affect personality development. Many people who develop dissociative disorders have family histories of habitual, overwhelming and life-threatening events at a critical stage of childhood.

Dissociation also occurs with constant neglect or emotional abuse, even when physical or sexual abuse is not a factor. Findings show that in families where parents are frightening and unpredictable, the children may become dissociative.

Shocked. This described our lives. My body erupted in chills.

*Dissociative identity disorder is diagnosed when the presence of
two or more distinct personalities take over a person's behavior.*

I dry swallowed. Take over the person's behavior?

*The different personalities, have their own age, sex, or race.
Each has his or her own postures, gestures and distinct way
of talking. When the personality shows itself and controls the
person's behavior and thoughts, it's called "switching." Switching
can take anywhere from seconds, to minutes, to days.*

*The dominant or primary personality is unaware of the 'alters'.
However, the 'alters' are acutely aware of the primary personality and their thoughts and feelings. The 'alters' exist because of
the primary personality's need.*

The descriptions fit how Jessie acted exactly: she moved like a different person, she used different terms and her face appeared harder or
older somehow. My entire body slumped over my desk. Was this the
twin the psychic had talked about?

CHAPTER 26

JESSIE

After many frustratingly short make-out sessions, Alex and I would be without parental supervision for the evening. All the stars must have aligned to allow such an event. Ally's parents were going out, as were Topher's who were attending a wedding and would be gone for several hours.

According to plan, Ally and I lay on the family room floor in our sweats, no makeup on, to convince her parents we were in for the night.

"Oh my God, I can't stand it another minute. Why won't my parents leave? Topher just texted me again and said about twenty people have arrived." She sighed, stared down at her phone, and texted Topher at a furious pace. I had no idea how she could type that fast. I thought it odd I hadn't had a text from Alex in two hours.

I texted him that I couldn't wait to see him, then frowned at my phone after a minute or two passed with no response. He usually responded quickly. Ally banged her head against the back of the cushioned couch repeatedly.

"Calm down. Your parents will leave at some point. I saw your Mom with her heels on, so they're going. If we look agitated, they may guess something is up."

"Look at this." She shoved her phone in front of my face. Topher's latest text said, "Baby, get over here right now. Have your parents left? Sneak out now!"

"He's losing his mind," I said.

"Me too," Ally groaned.

I looked at my phone again. Eight pm.

"Girls, we're heading out now. Call us if anything comes up," said Ally's mom, adjusting an earring in the hall mirror.

"Okay," Ally said.

I just kept my eyes glued to my phone. As soon as they closed the door, we ran to the bathroom to get ready.

Thirty minutes later, we walked up to Topher's house. The bass vibrated through the walls. Ally and I looked at each other wide-eyed. We didn't need to discuss the party. We both knew it was out of control.

We let ourselves in via the back door. Our classmates had packed themselves into the house wall to wall. Solo cups of who knows what were passed out by a very happy senior.

"Ladies, would you like a beverage?" The polite question came from a burly football player who wore his jersey with the number twenty-two proudly displayed.

"I'm good, twenty-two. Thanks, though." I grinned at him but scanned the party for Alex, who still hadn't responded to my texts. We found Topher in the living room, involved in a game of beer pong.

"Suck on that!" he yelled to his opponents as we approached, jumping up and throwing his hands over his head. I assumed he was winning, but I don't think it mattered.

He spotted Ally and hurried toward her with arms spread wide.

"You're here! Finally...I didn't know if your parents were *ever* going to leave," he said. A vertical wrestling match ensued as he hugged Ally and inadvertently put all his weight on her. She struggled to hug him back and hold him upright.

I didn't know how they'd gotten this drunk in an hour or two, but based on his goofy smile and shouted greeting, he was toast. I didn't see Alex anywhere.

"Topher, where's Alex?" I said.

He looked at me with his glazed eyes, "Probably playing cards upstairs. Why don't you sit down, and I'll go get him?"

"Okay," I said.

I started to sit down with Ally, but then changed my mind. My gut told me something wasn't right.

"I'll be right back." I followed Topher, who didn't notice me casually tracking him as he climbed the stairs and turned the corner to go down the hall.

"Alex! Jessie is here," Topher said.

My heart dropped to my stomach when I heard his tone. I turned the corner just a few seconds later. Alex leaned against the wall, with a girl pressed against him. They were kissing. It was Amanda. He held a cup in one hand and his other hand gripped her ass.

Topher turned to see me directly behind him. He mumbled, "Oh shit." Pain ripped through my body and triggered something inside me.

CHAPTER 27

THE OTHER

I wanted to kill them both. I strode toward them. Alex pushed Amanda away from him.

"It's a little late for that, don't you think?" My hand on my hip and my legs slightly spread, I stared them down. They both wore expressions of drunken confusion. Alex put his head in his hands.

To Amanda, I said, "Leave." I would allow her to walk away.

"I don't have to leave just because you showed up," she sneered. "And this isn't the first time we've done this." She motioned with her thumb to indicate her and Alex.

She made the grave mistake of giving me a smart-assed smile. I hate smart-asses.

I leaned slightly toward my right, turned my body and drove my left foot into her midsection. Her stomach squished under my shoe. Alex tried to grab and pull me to him, but I easily avoided his efforts. Amanda stumbled down the hall, doubled over.

While Alex yelled at Topher for bringing me upstairs, I followed her into Topher's room. I could see the dull anger in her eyes as she lunged toward me. Stupid, silly girl. I deflected her hand and smashed my fist into her nose. Her nose crunched under my knuckles and blood ran down her face.

She held her nose. "Look at what you've done, I'm bleeding," she sobbed.

I grabbed her by the hair and drew my fist back for another punch. Damn, I loved this party.

"Jessie, stop!" Alex wrapped his arms around me and pinned my arms to my side.

Amanda half crawled, then stood up and ran from the room.

"I'm sorry. I didn't want this, she started kissing me," he said.

With his arms still wrapped around me, I leaned forward and drove my foot up and into his balls. I felt them collapse under my heel.

He dropped to the floor. Stupid asshole. I leaned over him. "I hope for your sake you like her a lot, because you just ruined your chances with us. You will never get the privilege of touching us ever again. You're disgusting," I said.

"Please." His eyes squeezed shut. "I didn't want that to happen."

"Whatever. We're done with you." The image of him with his hand on her ass was something we would never forget.

"Jessie!" Ally called as she ran down the hallway.

I walked out of the bedroom and caught her before she barreled into me. Everyone called me Jessie; it annoyed me.

"What's going on?" Ally said as she looked at me and then Alex on the floor. "Amanda said you punched her."

"I gave her the option to leave." I shrugged. "She's not a smart girl."

"Okay," Ally said slowly. She couldn't take her eyes off Alex. "What did you do to him?"

"Nothing he didn't deserve. Let's go get a drink," I said.

"I thought you didn't drink?" she said, lifting her eyebrows. We walked back downstairs.

"Well, I do tonight. Let's celebrate. I just dumped Alex." I assumed Miss Bloody Nose had left the party. Good thing, because the energy surging through me needed to be directed somewhere. As I walked down the stairs, all eyes were on me.

"Hey, number twenty-two, hook me up. I'm ready for a drink now," I said.

"Fantastic," he said and handed me a cup. "Don't tell your brother I gave you a drink. He would kill me."

I winked at him, then grabbed the drink and downed it. It was clear alcohol with fruit juice. The alcohol burned down my throat. There seemed to be very little fruit juice mixed in.

I coughed a little and said, "Wow, no wonder you guys are drunk." This comment garnered high fives and laughter from my classmates. I grabbed another cup and downed that one too. The liquor pumped through my body like wildfire. Alex came down the steps with a look of devastation on his face. He reached for my hand. I jerked it away and pushed him hard against his chest. He stumbled back a few steps.

"Don't touch us again," I snarled.

Topher grabbed his arm and pulled him into the kitchen.

I studied the room and my eyes landed on Will. I liked Will. I liked tall blondes specifically. He stood with his back against the family room wall. Perfect.

He watched as I walked up to him.

"Kiss me." I got to the point. I knew the better man, and it was Will. Jessie didn't see it as clearly.

He smiled and said, "What?"

"Kiss me," I repeated without breaking eye contact. I stepped closer to him.

He studied me another second and then put down his cup. He put his fingers under my jaw and tilted my face up to his. He gazed into my eyes questioning, but ran his thumb over my lips wiping off the lip gloss.

"Not a fan of lip gloss, I guess?" My lips were inches from his.

"Nope." He lowered his lips to mine. His breath became my breath.

He kissed me tentatively at first, but all the energy I had bottled up surged into him. I kissed him thoroughly, and wrapped my arms around his neck. His arms circled around my waist and pressed me against him. His lips fit perfectly with mine. We kissed each other for a long time it seemed. The alcohol added fuel to my desire. We may have gone on for hours, but boys started shouting behind us.

Will lifted his head and we both looked to see what was happening. Topher and a few other boys restrained Alex. Alex, wild-eyed and deranged, struggled to get away.

"I will kill you!" he shouted at Will.

"You should leave, man. This is nuts," Topher said as he held Alex around the waist.

"Sure, no problem." Will smiled at Alex, spread his hands wide and said, "Any time, Alex, just let me know."

Alex renewed his efforts. "This isn't over!"

I interrupted before he could get away. "You know what? I'll leave." I raised my hands in exasperation.

"Let me walk you out," Will said.

"No, I don't think that's a good idea. I'll catch you later," I said.

He stepped toward me and kissed me softly on the lips. "You will," he said.

As I walked to the door, I looked back at Alex. He stared at me. I flipped him off and walked out the door, laughing.

CHAPTER 28

JESSIE

Snowflakes drifted gently to the ground. The woods were quiet and dim. I held out my hand and watched the flakes melt as they hit my skin. Snow clung to the branches of the trees.

Where was I? I didn't panic. My emotions existed on another level. I looked toward the source of light and recognized the back of Ally's house. Realization dawned, I was sitting in the small woods located at the back of her property. My phone started to buzz in my jacket pocket. I reached for it, but before I could Ally appeared out of nowhere.

"Where have you been? I've been looking for you for hours," she said.

"Alex made out with Amanda," I said. The thought persisted in my mind as the most important thing I needed to say.

"I know." Her brows furrowed as she reached down to help me up.

"Come on, let's get back to the house." She put her arm around my waist. "Why didn't you answer my phone calls? I had to pretend we were in bed asleep when my parents came home." She waved her hands, punctuating her words, and then raised them heavenward and said, "Thank God my mom didn't look closely."

"I didn't hear my phone." Tears flowed down my face. My frozen butt made movement painful. We snuck back into the house and quietly crept to Ally's bedroom.

"I started to follow you when you left, but Topher asked me to help him pick up the house. We kicked everyone out before his parents got home. I thought you would go back to my house," she said.

"I'm sorry."

"It's okay. I can't believe Alex made out with Amanda. I'm serious, she's gross." Ally lay back on the bed and heaved a big sigh. "What a mess."

"Yes," I said.

The last thing I remembered was Alex in the hallway kissing Amanda. I felt detached from my body and emotions. The tidal wave loomed above me without breaking. It would come soon enough. I would cherish the numbness for as long as it lasted.

"Well, you're a legend after tonight's performance," Ally said.

"What do you mean?" I frowned.

"Out of all of the shit you pulled? Where do I start? First off, no one could believe you punched Amanda in the face. Second, you kicked Alex in the nuts and dumped him. And third, for the grand finale, you made out with Will in front of the whole party. Topher almost lost his mind trying to keep Alex from killing Will."

I made out with Will? What in the hell was I thinking?

"You did so many crazy things, it's hard to say which is the biggest topic of conversation."

The knowledge of my actions stung my shocked brain. My mind cycled through what I could remember. The memory of Alex kissing Amanda tore at my heart. I didn't remember anything after that until the woods. Tears continued to roll down my cheeks.

"Did you think he loved me?" I needed to understand why this happened.

"Yeah, he acted like he adored you," Ally said, biting her lip.

"Did you see something with Alex and I that I didn't notice?" My butt began to thaw. I wiggled around to get comfortable.

"No, I thought you were great together."

"I don't understand." With all this drama, I appreciated my friends even more. I trusted them with my raw emotion.

"I know. It doesn't make any sense. I don't know why some guys can behave themselves and others can't," Ally said.

"I love him, and I know he loves me. Why would he do this?" I stared at her in desperation. "I thought if they loved you, they didn't mess around with other girls." My bottom lip quivered.

"I think that way too. I guess you never know." She wiped her eyes—when one of us cried, we all did.

I sobbed into my hands. Ally scooted over and put her arms around me. Why is it when someone hugs you, it makes you cry harder?

I got up to go to the bathroom and blow my nose. My eyes were swollen, as was my red face, but the true centerpiece was my nose, which appeared twice its normal size. Pain pulsed through my brain in time with every heartbeat. I came back from the bathroom and crawled into bed.

"Let's go to sleep. I can't think about this anymore," I said.

"Yeah, I'm exhausted too," Ally said mid-yawn.

I lay down and thought I would be awake for a while, but gratefully slipped into oblivion.

Gray daylight seeped into Ally's room, penetrating my swollen eyelids. I glanced at my phone; it read ten am. I rolled over to see Ally still sleeping. I quietly got up, dressed and made my way to the bathroom. If I thought I looked bad last night, I clearly didn't understand how bad it could get. I ran cold water and cupped my hands under the faucet. I rinsed my face and held the cold water against my eyes and cheeks. I did this repeatedly until some of the swelling went down. My phone buzzed in my purse. I picked it up to see a text from Brian saying he would be there in twenty minutes to pick me up. I took a deep breath. He probably knew about the party.

Normally, I wouldn't bother with makeup on the weekend, but my red, swollen face required it. I patted and rubbed some foundation on to mask the redness, then smudged on some eyeshadow and a little mascara. In the mirror, I appeared marginally better. I grabbed my things and walked to the front door.

"Thanks for having me over." I waved to Ally's parents, who were drinking coffee at the kitchen table. I didn't want them to get a close look at my face.

"Can I make you breakfast?" Ally's mom asked.

"No thank you. Brian is here to pick me up." I waved and left.

My phone buzzed. I looked down at the message. It was from Alex. He had texted me all night and filled my voicemail. I turned the sound off and put it back in my purse. My emotional numbness lingered, but I knew devastation lurked below.

I walked out to Brian's car and the frigid air soothed my face.

Brian pounced as soon as I got in. "What the hell happened at Topher's party last night? At least five people texted me about you." His face creased in tension and worry. "You look awful."

"I saw Alex making out with Amanda," I said.

"I heard. He's a douchebag; you're better off without him." He gripped the wheel. "I heard a lot more happened. Do you want to tell me?"

"That's all I remember." I looked at my hands folded in my lap.

"Were you drunk?" He ran his hand back through his hair and stared straight ahead blankly.

"No." I rolled my eyes.

"Nothing at all?" Brian persisted.

"The last thing I remember is seeing Alex kissing Amanda," I said.

"I heard you punched Amanda in the face. Do you realize she could press charges?" He gave me a sidelong glance. "The only reason she won't is because she doesn't want her parents to know she was at a party last night."

"If you already know what happened, why are you asking me then?" He made me mad.

"I needed to know if you knew what happened." He tapped the steering wheel repeatedly.

I rubbed my forehead. I didn't remember any of those things. "What's wrong with me?" I rocked back and forth. Was this related to what the gypsy said? My dark twin?

"Remember you told me Mrs. Palmer mentioned dissociative disorder to you," he said.

"Yes."

"I looked it up. It happens to people who have grown up as abused kids, like us. I don't know if I understand it completely, but it sounds like you have other personalities called alters. The alter personalities deal with parts of your life you can't handle."

A tingling sensation enveloped me. It started in my head and traveled down my body. What he said felt true. My ears rang.

I blinked and shook my head. "The gypsy was right. I do have a dark twin."

"No, she's crazy. That was all bullshit," Brian said.

"It's not bullshit! She's right!" I yelled.

I rubbed my face and tried to bring back some feeling. "I'm scared." I felt the fear to the depth of my soul. "I don't know what to do."

"Stress, fear or anger triggers it. You have to remain calm. It wouldn't be good if you went into one of these fits at school."

"What am I going to do?" I said.

"You're going to stay calm. This will pass. We've been through a lot lately…once things settle down you'll be okay."

"Okay. I can stay calm." I trusted Brian above all others. If he said it would be okay, then it would be.

My brain ached with too many problems. It hurt to breathe, but the minutes relentlessly ticked along. Life was like that sometimes, brutal in its continuity.

As we pulled in our driveway, I practically jumped out of the car. I needed some air. I needed to move. "Tell Mom I'm going over to Rebecca's for an hour or so."

"Okay," Brian muttered.

I walked toward her house, but continued past it. I wanted to walk until I was exhausted. I shoved my hands into my pockets and strode down the street with my head down.

The cool breeze lifted my hair but didn't have the bite of winter to it. The snow last night had quickly melted, and spring was starting to make its appearance in the new patches of fresh green grass. It made me feel better to see the flower buds pushing through the soil. Something about the outdoors always soothed me.

After an hour, I made my way back home. Maybe the exercise would help me relax. I laughed to myself; this is why people drank, to forget. I entered the house via the garage and went into the kitchen.

"Hey, sweetie, how was your night?" Mom asked.

"Fine. We stayed up late watching movies so I'm tired. Got to go to the bathroom," I said.

I moved past her and into the bathroom. I shut the door and studied my face. It appeared less swollen. I didn't want her to ask me if something was wrong.

For the rest of the day, I sat with Brian and watched—or pretended to watch—football. My phone buzzed for the tenth time and Brian plucked it from my hand.

"Give it back!" I reached for it, but he held it in his other hand away from me.

"Stop. I need to do something." His face told me he wasn't joking around. "I'm keeping your phone for tonight. You'll want to talk to him and he'll try to wiggle his way back together with you. You're done with that kid. Do you understand me?"

My nails looked ragged in my lap. I couldn't stop picking at them. "Yes, I get it."

"You can't let him treat you that way and take him back." He furiously typed a text and then seemed satisfied after it sent. "I'm still going to keep your phone for tonight."

I balled my hands into fists. "Whatever Brian, I get it. You're the boss." I stomped back to my room.

Leaning against the door, I scrubbed my face with my hands. What could Alex possibly be saying via text that would change anything? The world was the same, but for me, all the joy had disappeared. As much as I wanted him back in my life, I wouldn't take him back. Brian was right; I would not be a fool for a guy. But what did I have to offer anyway? I was defective. I shuddered at the long road of nothingness ahead of me.

I went into the bathroom, washed my face and brushed my teeth. Today had been the longest day of my life. I crawled into bed and lay on my back. Out my window stood one of the two large silver maple trees my parents had planted twenty years before. The boughs now towered over our roof, like two sentinels guarding the house. They'd served as our base for games of tag and keep away. The gray branches were bare now and swayed slightly in the cold wind. I imagined myself as the tree; my hair and arms hardened into the upper branches, my face, neck and body ingrained into the trunk, my legs and feet roots digging deep into the earth. Just like the tree, I existed cold and bare, miserably alone in the dark.

I rolled onto my side and whispered, "Good night, Alex."

Dreamless sleep was my only reward.

CHAPTER 29

JESSIE

Monday morning sucked. I dreaded going back to school. My hair steamed under the straightener. Brian's knock on the open bathroom door distracted me. He leaned against the doorway. "I'll take you and Rebecca to school today."

"Okay. Thanks." I put the straightener down and texted her, so she knew we had a ride. I was surprised he'd offered. He liked having that time alone with Tracey. At least I wouldn't have to see Alex first thing. Plus, getting a ride with Brian was a lot nicer than riding the bus. We pulled into Rebecca's driveway and she jogged to the car with a big smile on her face.

"Thanks for the ride," she said as she got in the backseat with me. Her eyes sparkled with her smile.

I leaned toward the front seat. "You know you could give us a ride every day."

"Uh huh," he mumbled.

He didn't even look at me when I asked. I sat back in my seat, looked at Rebecca and shrugged. We enjoyed the ride anyway. As we pulled into the parking lot, I scanned the crowd to see who was around. Tim stood near his car waiting for Brian.

As soon as I got out, Tim put his arm around me and squeezed, like a side hug. "How's it going, beaver?"

I cringed at the nickname. "Fine."

He put his arm around Rebecca too and pulled us both slightly off the ground. "Come on ladies, let's go get educated."

Brian rolled his eyes and shook his head. Rebecca and I giggled. Tim was always a lot of fun. He walked into school with us.

"Catch ya later." He winked at Rebecca. Her checks flushed red.

"I love him," she whispered to me.

I laughed. "I bet you do, and dare I say the feeling is mutual?"

"Shut up!" Rebecca said.

We parted ways for our respective lockers. My lingering smile disappeared as I turned the corner and saw Alex standing at mine. Kristi and Ally were at theirs as well.

"We'll wait for you," Kristi said.

I heaved a huge sigh and walked up to my locker. Alex looked awful. His eyes were bloodshot, and his clothes looked like he'd slept in them.

I ignored him as I entered my code. He put his arms on either side of me and leaned his head into the back of mine and whispered, "Please talk to me. I'm so sorry. I have no excuse for my behavior. I love you."

I stood still and listened to his voice and his words. His warm breath on the back of my neck provided the oxygen I needed. I closed my eyes and focused on remembering his closeness. All I wanted was for him to hold me and comfort me. I physically ached. I took a deep breath and opened my eyes. Kristi and Ally stood a few feet away, waiting for me.

I knew if I looked into his eyes, I would be lost. I turned toward him but didn't make eye contact. I started to say *I love you too* but stopped myself. He'd betrayed me brutally and publicly. What was I thinking? Anger swelled inside me.

"Stop calling me and don't come around me again. You ruined everything. Would you take me back if I did that to you?" I put my hand on my hip and waited for his answer.

"You made out with Will," he said, exasperated.

"Payback is a bitch."

He stared at me wide-eyed and then hung his head. I wanted to leave, but couldn't make my feet move. Ally saved me by stepping forward and holding her hand out. Alex however, grabbed my other hand.

"Please, let me make it up to you," he pleaded.

I kept my eyes on Ally's face. She glared at him and raised her eyebrow.

"Brian, don't!" Tracey yelled.

I turned to see my brother slam Alex into the row of lockers.

"What did I fucking tell you?" he said, baring his teeth. Alex's shirt was clutched in his fists. "Touch her again and I'll kill you."

"I just wanted to talk to her...that's all..."

I stood glued to the floor. I looked over at Tracey, but she held her hand over her mouth. Coach Wilson appeared out of thin air.

"Gentlemen. Do we have a problem here?" He barked the question.

"No." Brian slowly released Alex's shirt from his grip, and his face began returning to its normal color.

"Let's take a walk. The rest of you get to class." Coach Wilson indicated an open classroom to Brian.

Alex looked at me for a moment, then walked the other direction. A small crowd had gathered around us.

Tracey and I locked eyes in mutual anxiety.

"We can't do anything now, so let's just go to class," she said, and shrugged.

"Okay." We both looked the direction Brian had gone. Tracey gave me a brief hug and said she'd catch up with me later.

Ally and Kristi escorted me to homeroom. I was grateful for their presence.

"Wow. That was intense." Ally shook her head in disbelief. "I'm awake now. I have to say it; your brother is so hot! Those muscles and that bad-boy temper. Yum."

I snorted. "You're crazy. Seriously."

We took our seats. I got out my English book and started reading our next assignment. My mind needed to be occupied with other things. The first bell rang, and Holly came over to my desk to walk to class.

"I'm going to wait until the last minute and then come to class. Okay?"

"Sure," she said, lightly squeezing my shoulder. I could see the pity in her eyes, which made me feel worse. I stopped around the corner from my classroom, the chill from the cement wall seeping through my shirt as I leaned against it. The second bell rang, and only then did I finish the walk to class.

I avoided the places where Alex and I used to meet. My day was a mechanical routine. A black cloud of grief engulfed me as Alex haunted my every thought. His drinking, his betrayal...I thought he loved me. My body and my mind were broken glass.

. . .

Each day of school dragged, but I looked forward to track practice. Running and fresh air would give me some distraction from my sadness. Even though Amanda was on the team, I easily avoided her—she ran distance and I ran sprints, and the two groups didn't practice much together. Rebecca was waiting for me at my locker.

"Hey, how's it going?" She eyed me suspiciously.

"Let's not talk about it." I took a deep breath and released it. She nodded. I kept my eyes on the floor as we walked toward the girl's locker room.

"Eat this, we have to get you going," She handed me a candy bar. I gave her a small smile. "Chocolate fixes everything," she said.

"I wish."

Coach Wilson stood in front of the gym. "Girls, hurry up. You need to be on the bus in twenty minutes." We hurried into the locker room to change. Our first track meet of the season was today. I had managed to avoid Will so far, but today it would be impossible. And to make things even worse, Alex and Will would be together.

Clothes changed, we loaded into the school buses for the short ride to the other school.

Centerville's high school was built on a large expanse of flat land. Bare trees surrounded the track in an otherwise empty field. Sparse bleachers were set up on opposite sides of the field.

As I stepped off the bus, the cool wind slapped my hair against my face. I pulled it into a pony tail and secured it with the hair tie on my wrist. The guys got off their bus and headed to the field. I scanned the guys and frowned when I didn't see Alex. I did, however see Will. He broke into a huge smile when our eyes met. I couldn't hold back an answering smile to his infectious grin. Something within me responded to him. I couldn't explain it.

We filed into the bleachers and put our bags and equipment down. I jogged out to the field and jumped around trying to get my blood flowing. Mentally, I had to prepare for the three hundred-meter hurdles, which were basically a form of torture. The hurdles were already in place on the track. Jitters invaded my stomach. We would have to run almost a lap of the track and jump over eight hurdles along the way. I dreaded this race. I stripped down to my uniform. Why we competed in tank tops and tiny shorts was beyond me. It wasn't warm until late in the season.

"You ready for this?" I asked. My teammate and fellow hurdler, Patty, walked beside me to the starting line.

"As ready as I possibly can be," she said. "Good luck."

"Thanks." I queued up for the race. I would run in the first heat.

I settled myself into the starting block and casually eyed my competition. I didn't recognize any of the other runners, so I assumed they were older. My stomach rolled, and my legs shook slightly as I kneeled into position.

The announcer counted off and *bang*, we all ran for the first hurdle. Nerves and adrenaline propelled me forward. I flew over the track with my light cleats. The track was springy, which gave me an additional boost. The first five hurdles were doable, but by the sixth, my legs were tired and my breath labored. I pushed hard with my back leg and sailed over the sixth hurdle a little lower than normal. My trailing leg skimmed the top of the seventh, but by the eighth I wondered if I'd be able to get my numb legs to cooperate. I jumped, but my trailing knee hit the hurdle with a bang and knocked it over. My arms pin wheeled for balance. One girl passed me as I struggled. I righted myself to finish the race.

Breathing heavily, I dragged myself off the track to the grass. Patty low-fived me as I passed her.

"Good run," she said.

"Thanks," I panted. "Good luck."

"Thanks." She started to jog over to the starting line but turned back. "Hey, cheer me on at the end so I don't die out."

I nodded. Still panting, I continued to pace around the field until my heart rate came down.

She headed over to the blocks for her race. I stood between the sixth and seventh hurdles. Even with my hair in a ponytail, the wind continued to smack strands against my face. The announcer gave the signal for the next race. Will sidled up to me.

"Good run," he said.

"Thanks."

The starting gun sounded. I watched as Patty smoothly glided over the first few hurdles.

"She's doing great."

"Yeah, she's got great endurance. Her gymnastics training helps."

He gazed adoringly at me; with his light blond hair, he looked like an angel.

Patty approached so I cupped my hands around my mouth to cheer for her. "Come on Patty! Keep coming."

She struggled to clear the seventh hurdle. Her trailing knee hit, and she began to fall. To my amazement, she tucked in her arms and legs and fell into a front roll, then popped right back up and kept running. Will and I gaped at each other.

"Oh my God. That was incredible! I can't believe she rolled out of the fall." My eyes were wide.

"I know!" Will said.

I remembered to shut my mouth after a minute. We just stood there smiling and staring at each other for several seconds.

Oblivious to the cool wind, we ran across the field. We had to see her finish the race.

She cleared the last hurdle and crossed the finish line. We all gathered around her.

"That was amazing, kid." Coach Wilson enthused. "What a recovery. I've never seen anything like it."

"It just happened. I didn't even think about it," she said, panting and smiling at the same time. "Guess gymnastics took over."

"Yeah…and good thing. You'd have track burn for sure," I said. "That was awesome!" I patted her back.

Coach Wilson looked at us and clapped his hands together. "Good job, ladies. Go get your gear on before you get too cold." We dispersed to get our stuff.

Will waited for me. "That was so cool," he said.

"Yeah, it sure was."

I wondered where Alex was for the fifth time.

"Did you hear about Alex?" Will asked, as if reading my mind.

"No, what?" I asked.

"He showed up drunk at practice today. Coach got a whiff of him and kicked him off the team."

My stomach dropped. I didn't want this for him.

"No! Why would he do that?" The information utterly depressed me.

"I don't know, obviously he's got some issues," said Will.

God, please help him. I didn't wish the life of a drunk on anyone.

Will walked me over to the bleachers, where I sat down and reached into my bag for my black sweatpants. I carefully eased them over my cleats and pulled them up over my shorts.

He sat beside me, his hands clasped together in front of him. His straight blond hair blew across his forehead in the wind. We sat in a comfortable silence watching our fellow teammates.

"I have to say your kiss at the party surprised me," he said.

Heat rushed to my face. "Yeah, me too," I said, thinking he had no idea just how much it surprised me or how, in fact, I didn't even remember it. "I'm sorry. I went a little crazy that night."

"No need to apologize. I enjoyed it," he said.

I rubbed my palms against my sweats. My heartbeat pounded in my ears. "I do like you. I mean obviously, I like you," I stammered, "but I need to get Alex out of my head first. It wouldn't be fair to you if I didn't."

"I understand." He locked his eyes to mine. "You should know you were always too good for him."

"Why, cause he was always gaming me?" I asked.

"Yeah, he's just a douchebag."

"I sort of figured that out, but it still hurts." I shrugged.

"You'll get over him. Time heals all wounds, right?" He put his arm around me and gave my shoulder a squeeze; I melted into his half hug.

"I hope so," I said.

"Friends for now?"

"Absolutely." I exhaled in relief. I wanted to be able to talk with him and hang out. Selfishly, I needed something to distract me from the continued grief over Alex.

"JESSIE!" Coach Wilson bellowed from the field, waving his hands urgently.

"Oh shit, my relay." I quickly took off my sweats. "I have to go."

Will grinned and waved me on.

I hurried down to the track. Rebecca, already on the field, gave me the stink eye with her palms spread wide. I caught up with her as we walked to our positions.

"Seriously?" she said.

I chuckled, "Sorry."

"Are you ready?" She studied me.

"It's a relay, it's not that hard. Chill."

"Just checking. See you in a few."

I stood at my relay point on the track and waited for the race to begin. Thoughts of Alex drinking depressed me; it didn't make any sense. *Bang!* The starting gun discharged. I readied myself to run, but this time, it wasn't for my life.

CHAPTER 30

BRIAN

"I hope you've had time to consider your actions from a few days ago."

Coach Wilson stared at me from across his desk.

"It won't happen again." I rubbed my fist in the palm of my left hand.

"Good to hear, because the next fight will get you suspended. And that's going to look really bad on your college applications," Coach said.

"Yeah, but that little shit is pushing it. I'm sure you heard what happened?" I said.

"Yes…but do you understand the consequences?" He leaned forward with his lips pressed into a hard line.

"Okay, I hear you."

"But, boy oh boy, sounds like your sister has a temper. It must run in the family."

"You could say that." He had no idea just how correct he was.

"Jessie can handle her own battles anyway," he said.

"Yeah," I mumbled, but I didn't agree.

"Good, now get your butt to class."

I still wanted to beat Alex's ass. Coach was right, though. I couldn't risk college on this douchebag.

Tracey stood at her locker talking to Tim, who whistled as I approached.

"Well Hello, Mr. Ass Kicker," he said. He stepped behind Tracey, pointed to her and mouthed, "You're in trouble."

"What did Coach have to say?" She glared up at me with her hand on her hip.

"He told me he would suspend me if I got into another fight."

"You can't do that shit again," she said.

Another thing I loved about Tracey, she told me what she thought, but she didn't nag. She fully expected my cooperation.

"I know."

She entwined her fingers with mine. "Come on, Mr. Ass Kicker, we have English."

I laughed; as Tim came up beside me, and I gave him a friendly shove. By the time class ended, my stomach was growling. Thank God I ate in the first lunch period.

Tracey waited in the salad line, which meant I arrived at our table first. Mechanically, I chewed my second hot dog. Taste didn't matter as much as quantity. Hunger was my constant companion. I scarfed down French fries and a chocolate milkshake in short order. Tracey sat down across from me and picked at her grilled chicken salad. I would eat that too, if she didn't want it.

My eyes scanned the lunchroom until I spotted Jessie. Good, she was sitting with the girls. Alex was nowhere in sight. As a drunk's kid, I was always aware of my surroundings, the entry and exit points of a room. A handy survival skill. It was critical to know when to run and where. Amanda and her buddies sat a few tables away. As I watched, she shot a dirty look in Jessie's direction. I stopped chewing, and swallowed.

"What are you staring at?" Tracey turned in her seat to follow my gaze. "Oh, no," she whispered.

She turned back, eyes wide. She'd judged the danger as clearly as I had. Even though I hadn't given her any details, I'd mentioned that my sister's behavior was unpredictable lately.

"Amanda can't be that stupid. Does she want another black eye?" Tracey whispered.

"Jessie better not touch her at school. They'll both get in trouble. Let's finish up and go over there," I said.

As we put our trays away, I kept my eyes trained on Jessie. She, Rebecca, Kristi and Ally had their heads close together and were talking quietly. Just as I put my tray on the conveyor belt, a chair scraped loudly against the tile.

Jessie had pushed herself back from the table. She glared at Amanda with fury in her eyes. Rebecca held out her hand, but Jessie ignored her. Brandishing her hot dog, she prowled over to Amanda's table. Oh shit, she'd lost it again. I jogged over, hearing Tracey's footfalls right behind me.

Amanda and her friends were openly hostile as Jessie stood there. Jessie threw her uneaten hotdog, minus the bun, in front of Amanda. Hard lines on either side of her mouth transformed her face. Rage rippled from her body in waves. Clearly, she was dangerous.

"Does that look familiar? I know you're a big fan of wieners," Jessie said.

My mouth hung open. Jessie sneered. Rebecca watched Jessie uncertainly. She must have felt the change. I edged around the table.

Amanda said nothing, and avoided Jessie's stare. Smart girl.

"Why don't you walk away? You aren't welcome here," one of Amanda's friends said.

Jessie turned her cold gaze on her. "Shut up, bitch." She flicked her fingers in a shooing gesture. "Be glad this doesn't concern you."

The girl cowered at Jessie's tone and the unhinged look in her eyes.

"What? You don't want the wiener?" Jessie said in a pouty voice. She leaned over in front of Amanda's face and placed her hands on the table. "You've had enough?"

"Jessie, stop." I snapped my fingers under her face. I couldn't think of anything else to do. Her dark eyes focused on me. There was no trace of my sister in her stare.

"Stay out of this," she said.

Jessie never talked to me that way.

Still in Amanda's face, she said, "Pray you don't cross my path. I won't hold back again. Slut." She threw the empty bun at Amanda.

She stalked away without a backward glance, again with the grace of a cat.

"What the hell set her off?" I asked Rebecca.

"Kristi told Jessie that she heard Alex had been sleeping with Amanda for weeks before the party. Jessie turned completely white, then shoved back her chair." My concern was reflected in her eyes.

"Brian, Mrs. Palmer just stopped Jessie," whispered Tracey from behind me.

The day had escalated out of control in a five-minute time span. I rushed over to them. Mrs. Palmer held Jessie's elbow and studied her face.

Mrs. Palmer was trying to get Jessie to tell her what was wrong. Jessie looked at her and jerked her elbow out of Mrs. Palmer's hand.

"Hey, I can take it from here. She's upset over her boyfriend." I smiled at Mrs. Palmer and hoped I could talk our way out of this.

"Thanks, Brian, but I would like to speak with her." She pointed Jessie toward the exit sign.

"Jessie, come with me to my office. We can talk for a few minutes."

Helplessly, I watched them walk away. There was nothing I could do.

"Do you think she is going to get in trouble?" said Tracey. She frowned and watched their retreating figures.

"I don't know." I sighed and put my arm around her. "I'm going to wait outside her office for Jessie. I'll catch up with you later." I squeezed her shoulder briefly and then hurried after them.

CHAPTER 31

THE OTHER

I jerked my elbow away from Mrs. Palmer's hand, but continued to walk with her. Her body stiffened, and she stepped away from me. I didn't know how Jessie stood school. We walked into Mrs. Palmer's office and I plopped down in a seat.

She studied my face. "What's going on right now? You're upset."

"Seriously? That bitch slept with our boyfriend. I mean our ex-boyfriend. So, hell yes, we're upset, angry, agitated, you name it."

"You said we. Who else is involved?"

"That's none of your business."

"I understand why you would be angry." She took a sip from the water bottle on her desk. "Is there anything you would like to tell me?"

I didn't like the way she was studying our face.

"What would you like to hear?" I said in a sarcastic tone.

Surprised, she leaned back in her chair. I liked watching her compose her features back into her professional mask.

"Do you remember when I mentioned I volunteered at the Veterans Association Hospital?"

"So?"

"Some of the veterans have post-traumatic stress disorder from serving in the war. It's caused by the tremendous amount of stress they endure. You appear to be experiencing similar symptoms."

"Really? And what symptoms are those?" I gave her my eat-shit smile. My arm hung casually over the back of the adjoining chair.

She looked me in the eye and started rattling them off. "Headaches, amnesia, lost time, and one you have mentioned to me called an out-of-body experience."

She paused for a moment and then continued. "Some people also have a tendency toward hurting themselves or others." She watched our face intently. "I've spoken with Jessie many times, but I don't think that's who you are. Who am I speaking with now?" she asked.

I chuckled. Well, well, well. Mrs. Counselor knows some things. I sat up in my chair and leaned closer to her desk.

"Ding, ding. I like you." It made me happy to know someone recognized my presence. "You know your stuff, but do you really think I'm going to answer that question?" Damn, it was entertaining to mess with her.

"I would like you to." She waited patiently.

"I can tell you a few things. I'm never going to let Alex or Amanda see how hurt Jessie is again." With my forearms on my knees, my eyes burned into hers. "Do you understand her level of despair?"

"Let me help you," she pleaded. She reached a hand across her desk.

"I don't need help. And you can't help her." My voice was flat and emotionless. The bell rang.

I stood. "Time's up. Sorry, Doc, but I have to go." I walked out of her office quickly. Did she think I would talk with her? We agreed with Brian not to share our issue with anyone else. If I was anything, I was loyal.

Brian was waiting for me outside the office. As soon as he saw me, he hurried over. "We're going home," he said.

"Why? I don't want to go home." I'd just thought of something. The hot guy, Will, from the party was here. I demanded a rematch. "Isn't Will here?" My mood zoomed from one direction to another. One minute enraged, the next interested in finding a guy.

"Oh, no, no, no. You're sick and I need to take you home," Brian said bluntly while herding me to the student parking lot.

"Now that you mention it, my head does hurt." I stumbled, but Brian steadied me. "Before I forget to tell you, Mrs. Palmer knows about me." I couldn't stay long. The energy I required quickly tired Jessie. It took a lot of adrenaline and blood flow to supply the strength and aggression I needed to function.

"What do you mean?" Anxiety creased his face. He put his hand on the wall.

"She knows I'm not Jessie," I said.

"Oh, God." He swallowed.

"Not God. Lena. My name is Lena," I chuckled.

He stared, his mouth hanging open. "Lena? That's your name? You have a separate name?"

"Yes."

"Does Jessie know you?" he asked.

"No. She isn't aware of me on a conscious level." This was fun. I liked talking to Brian.

"Let's get out of here. I need to sit down." He hurried toward the school exit.

We walked to the student parking lot and got into the car. Brian drove just a few miles away from school and then pulled over.

"I can't tell Jessie about you. I can barely handle it; I know she can't." He laid his forehead against the steering wheel. "Why are you here? How did this happen?" he asked.

"I exist to endure what Jessie can't. I will ensure she survives our father." I looked at him intently. "Don't worry, I'll keep you out of it."

"Are there more of you?" he asked.

"That's not your concern," I said.

His face took on a green tinge. He twisted in his seat and vomited out the window. Good thing he had rolled it down to get some air.

"Gross." I wrinkled my nose. "If you can't keep your shit together, I'm done talking."

"No, wait." He held his hand out. "Do you understand if people find out about you they will put Jessie in the nut house? You can't be noticeable to other people."

"I'll keep that in mind." I leaned back in my seat and closed my eyes.

"Don't go to sleep. I need to talk to you. What will you keep me out of?" He reached over and nudged my shoulder.

"Very few people can touch me and you're not one of them." I cracked one eye open to look at him. "I'm bored now and my head hurts. I'll talk when I want to."

I closed my eyes and felt the familiar sensation of falling back into place. Home existed in Jessie's heart and mind. As always, when I returned, Annie ran and jumped into my arms.

"I told you I wouldn't be gone long," I said.

"I know, but I don't want you to be gone any." Annie put her thumb into her mouth.

"Come on, no thumb-sucking. We talked about this." I adjusted her chubby little body on my hip and walked over to our place. Only one person could touch me and that was Annie, the baby in the family. Oh yeah, and Will. I liked Will.

CHAPTER 32

BRIAN

I sat slumped in my car. She completely shut down, just like flipping a switch. I put my head in my hands. What the hell was I going to do? What if Lena stayed and Jessie didn't come back? I tried to think how many times Lena might have shown up. Grandma's house, Topher's party, today at lunch...so three times. It was Lena who'd threatened Dad. She'd beat up Amanda and threatened to do it again. My mind spun with the possibilities. What if she threatened more people? I needed more information. I remembered some of the things I'd looked up on the internet, but talking to Lena was a reality check I didn't want.

Did treatment even exist? I pulled out my phone and searched for dissociative disorder on WebDocs. I scanned the information until I saw the treatment plan.

There was no cure? Great, just what I didn't want to know. Treatment would require long term counseling and medication for anxiety and depression. This sounded bad and intense.

I laid my head on the steering wheel. I told her I could fix this, but I was wrong.

I looked over at my sister. Her pale face and the purple circles under her eyes. She looked ill. Anger overcame me, and I pounded on the steering wheel. Why! Why! Why! How in the hell would we get past this?

"I'm sorry." I whispered to her sleeping form. My thoughts shot like machine gun fire around my brain. Grandma. I would have to tell her. She would make the right decisions for Jessie. Hopefully, Jessie wouldn't think I betrayed her. Who knew how Mom and Dad would react, but I didn't trust either of them to take care of her. It was their fault. I hated them both.

Grandma was visiting the next day. I would find a good time to talk to her then. The thought made me sick, like a rock in my stomach.

CHAPTER 33

JESSIE

A cool wind blew through the open car window onto my face. I opened my eyes, noticed bare trees and fields passing by. Sun streamed into the car; I squinted my eyes and leaned forward. I pressed the button to roll the window up.

"Jessie?" Brian eyeballed me cautiously as he drove.

"What?"

He let out his breath. "Thank God. I hoped you would come around." His hands relaxed their grip on the steering wheel.

"What time is it?" I asked.

"It's one-thirty. I said you were sick and took you out of school. You went nuts at lunch today."

He pulled off the road onto a dirt path that led to an abandoned barn. The barn roof folded inward and all the boards were gray. Dirt tire tracks cut through the tall grass.

Dread overtook me. I thought back to earlier today. The last thing I remembered was going to lunch with Rebecca. "I don't think I can stand hearing about it."

"You'll have to hear about it, because your friends will ask you about it. If it didn't involve you, I would think it was kind of funny, but it does involve you." Brian pushed his hair off his forehead. "You threw a hot dog, minus the bun, at Amanda and said something about how much she liked wien...."

On the word *wiener,* he started to laugh. Every time he tried to say the word he would get to 'wien' and not be able to finish the 'er' before exploding in hysterics. His face scrunched up, his shoulders shook, and tears squeezed out of the corners of his eyes.

"Seriously, you're killing me," he gasped.

I started to laugh as well. We both bent forward, clutched our midsections and shook with laughter.

Laughter, the sweetest release. All my tension evaporated for a glorious moment.

Brian wiped the tears from his face. "I forgot to mention one other thing. Mrs. Palmer watched your argument with Amanda and took you back to her office to talk. I waited for you. When you came out, before you were yourself, you said she knows about you."

"Like she knows I'm losing my mind?" I said.

"I guess."

"Oh shit, that's bad, really bad. Now what? What can we do?"

"It depends on what you said and if she is willing to do anything about it. I bet she won't do anything yet. You didn't talk to her that long. She'll want more information first," he said.

"This can't keep happening." I pressed my fingers to my temples.

"Don't overreact. Other than the threat to Dad, this is small potatoes. You fought with another girl over a guy. No biggie. Things will settle down. Okay?" he said, pushing for my agreement.

"I don't think things will settle down," I said quietly. I studied his face. He was lying to me. I could always tell.

"Stop. Don't say that. We can figure it out and we will."

I could feel him pushing his will into me. I wished I could absorb it, but it didn't work that way. He pressed his mouth into a grim line.

My life seemed as forlorn as the forgotten barn, surrounded by a field of brown grass. I would tell Grandma what was going on. She would know what to do. I leaned my head against the cold window glass. My head hurt, and I didn't want to think about this anymore.

"What are you thinking about?" Brian asked.

"Nothing important," I said, but I knew I needed to cut him loose. My problem would drag him down—and I wouldn't do that to him.

"I'm going to take you home and then I have to head back for weightlifting." He gently pushed my shoulder. "Come on, cheer up. It's not the end of the world. Go home and read one of your banned books or make brownies."

"Will do, Mr. Cheerleader," I said.

"Now that I think about it, make the brownies," he said.

"Of course." I tried to smile, and turn off what happened at school in my mind. I couldn't deal with it.

Brian dropped me off and I trudged into the house. In the kitchen, I got out the box of brownie mix. While I mixed the ingredients, I thought of Alex and wondered for the hundredth time why he would want to be with Amanda. I wished I could stop thinking about it. I couldn't turn this thought loop off. I knew he loved me. Up until the night of the party, he was so sweet. Not that I'm so fantastic, but I was prettier than Amanda. On the other hand, why would Amanda hook up with Alex? Alex was obviously dating me—we were together all the time, at school and out with friends. I wouldn't want to be some guy's secret hookup. I didn't get it on either side. Thank God things hadn't physically gone further with Alex. It would have made this hurt ten times more. My heart was raw and exposed.

I poured the brownie mix into the baking pan and put it in the oven. I licked the mixing spoon, never mind the raw egg. I could probably sit down and eat a bowl of brownie mix. The raw egg never made me sick. Knock on wood. With my luck, today would be the day.

My phone buzzed on the counter: Alex. He had stopped calling incessantly, but still called often. My hand hovered over the phone. I desperately wanted to hear his voice and return to my former life of being in love, but I couldn't go back. My hand closed into a fist. If I talked to him, I would never get over him. I made the choice—I would not be my mother. If someone treated me badly, we were done.

I changed into sweats. Thank God it was Friday. Even better, Dad was on second shift; I wouldn't see him until eleven pm, if at all. I pushed my worry down into the numb zone. I couldn't function otherwise. The oven timer dinged, and I set the brownies out to cool. Looking at the clock, I knew Rebecca would be home from school. I wrote a quick note to Mom to tell her where I was going and then left for Rebecca's house. A new outlet mall had opened, and I wanted Rebecca to go with us tomorrow. Grandma, Mom, Brian and I were going. If I stayed busy, I wouldn't think of Alex so much.

CHAPTER 34

JESSIE

M om turned around from the driver's seat to the back. "You settled in?"

"Yep, let the torture begin," Brian said.

I hit him in the shoulder.

"What? I'm only going because you won't pick out Tracey's birthday gift."

"You're right. You should pick out your girlfriend's gift." I made a face at him as I slumped down in my seat. Rebecca hadn't felt well this morning, so she decided to stay home. Shopping wouldn't be as fun without her. As we pulled out of the driveway, I could see Baby sitting behind the glass pane next to the front door. Her sad little face killed me. She watched us until I couldn't see her anymore.

"Did you bring your spending money?" Mom glanced at us via the rearview mirror.

"Yeah," I responded.

"Yes," Brian said.

I leaned forward in my seat and patted Grandma's shoulder. She laid her soft hand over mine. I gave her shoulder an additional pat and then sat back. The mall was twenty miles away so a nap was in order; I used my jacket as a pillow. The sounds of the car, the low radio music and Mom and Grandma's quiet conversation lulled me to sleep. Why was it so easy to fully relax while riding in a car?

Locked tires screamed against the pavement and startled me awake. Metal crashed into metal with a tremendous jolt. The impact initially pulled me away from the window only to slam my head back against it in the next second. Darkness and silence followed.

Warm trickles ran down my face. Time slowed down. My breath continued to fill my lungs and then exit. I blinked slowly. The car pinged and creaked as if in agony. My feet were wedged under something heavy. The realization hit; we'd crashed into something. My eyes flew wide and I jerked my head toward Brian. A burst of pain shot up my neck and into my head. He was slumped over in his seat, the car door pushed inward on his side. Blood trickled from his nose and his eyes were shut. I didn't see Mom or Grandma in the front seat and their car doors were open.

"No, No, No," I reached my hand to him and touched his head. I gently pushed his hair back, but no response. His head was warm. My seatbelt locked around me. I couldn't get any closer. Sobbing, I closed my eyes and sent my prayer/ demand heavenward. "God, please don't take him. He's all I have." As a last resort, I threatened God. "If you take him, I will follow. I won't live this life without him." I could handle a lot of things, but losing Brian would break me.

My car door jerked open. "Miss, are you okay?"

The paramedic sawed at my locked seatbelt, but I couldn't look away from Brian. I desperately looked for a sign of life, some response to my touch. I wanted to scream his name, but only a croaking sound emerged.

"Miss, are you okay?" the paramedic repeated. "We are going to get you out of the car."

I turned my head toward him.

"Him first," my voice cracked. My hand strained to stay in contact with Brain's head, but my strength had left me. My hand slipped away and so did my consciousness.

I experienced brief periods of awareness: the slamming of the ambulance doors, the EMT's cool, soft hand on my forehead and soothing assurances I would be okay. I opened my eyes and focused on her. "My brother?" I asked.

"I'm sure they are taking care of him. Let's get you feeling better," she replied.

My thoughts turned to Mom and Grandma. Where were they? Were they hurt?

Hours or days later, I heard two male voices near me. One was my dad's, but I didn't recognize the other. Someone's hand covered my hand and lightly patted it every so often. It was a hand I had held so many times before. Small and fine-boned, I had held it skipping along the sidewalk, sitting on the bus for kindergarten, and while getting in trouble. Rebecca.

My stomach rolled, and I turned my head to vomit. Rebecca let go of my hand and a nurse rushed over.

"It's okay. We'll get you cleaned up." The nurse pulled the privacy curtain into place. "Let's take that gown off and I'll help you put on a clean one."

She unsnapped the dirty gown and pulled it away, then put a clean one over my head and quickly jerked it into place. She gave me a drink of water and then added clean, warm blankets, pulling them up to my chin.

"Thank you," I said.

"You're welcome, honey." She left the room and Rebecca came back in.

Fully awake after the wipe down, I sat forward as Rebecca adjusted the bed and gave me more water.

"Thank you." My voice sounded weak. "Brian?"

"He's okay. He broke his leg, sustained a concussion and possibly damaged his spleen…they're running more tests to figure it out. If all goes well, he should be discharged in a few days. Your Grandmother has a concussion too, like you, but with her age she is having a little more trouble. Your mom broke her hip and bruised her arm and face. She's in the most serious condition. They took her for surgery. She's bleeding internally and they're not sure where."

Tears slid down my cheeks. Rebecca handed me a tissue.

"What happened?" I asked.

"Your mom turned on the green arrow, but another car ran a red light and smashed into the side of your car. I don't know anything about the person in the other car."

My head ached like I could have never imagined. My eyes wouldn't stay open for any length of time. Spots of tightness and pain tingled on my face. I raised my hand slowly to feel my cheeks.

"You have a few cuts from glass. Nothing that will scar your face though. The plastic surgeon examined you while you slept. He said your skin had great elasticity, which sounded good. I have no idea what it means."

The amount of information overwhelmed me. If I tried to focus, my head hurt more. "My head is killing me."

Rebecca reached over me and pushed the nurse's button. Almost immediately, a friendly voice asked what I needed.

"Jessie's awake and she says her head really hurts."

"I'll be right down," the voice answered.

"Thank you," Rebecca said.

I smiled at Rebecca. "You'll rule the world someday." Efficient should have been her middle name.

"Hopefully," she said.

The nurse walked in. "Hi, Jessie. I'm Michelle. I'm going to give you a painkiller through your IV line. You'll be comfortable in a few minutes." She winked at me.

I watched her adjust the IV bag and then inject something into the tubing to administer the drug. Wow, she was right. My heart pumped the medication through my body taking away the pain, the absence of which made me aware of how bad it had been. I closed my eyes. Rebecca rubbed chap stick along my lips and applied lotion to my hands. She could read my mind—I hated having dry lips and hands. The nurses came in and shook me awake every so often and checked my eyes.

The next time awareness dawned, another day had passed. I could see blue sky and sunshine from my window. Dad was sitting by my bed holding my hand. I jerked my hand away.

"Don't touch me," I said.

He jerked his head and hand back. "What's wrong with you? I'm just trying to comfort you."

"Sorry. You startled me." I cleared my throat and made sure my covers were pulled up under my chin. I pressed my remote to elevate my head. "How's Mom?

"She's out of surgery and stable. They stopped the internal bleed-ing." He sat with his arms crossed tightly over his chest.

"That's good. When can she come home?" I asked.

"In a few days, maybe. Brian will probably be released then too. The doctor wants to monitor him another day or two. You're getting released today," he said.

"I'm the only one?" I avoided looking at him.

"Yes, unfortunately they want to keep them all for a few more days," Dad said.

My heart sank. Every minute he made me increasingly uncom-fortable. It wasn't better if he was sober; I hated him. No matter what happened, I would never be comfortable with him or seek his presence. I could happily live the rest of my life without ever seeing him again.

"Good, you're awake," Rebecca said as she walked in. "Hi, Mr. Taylor."

"Hi, Rebecca," Dad answered curtly and then stood. "I'm going to sign off on your paperwork, so get ready to leave."

"Okay." I looked down. I only wore a hospital gown.

"The doctor told me you would be released today," Rebecca said. "So, I brought you some clothes."

I sighed with relief. "Thank you."

She held out her hand and I slowly got out of bed. The room tilted slightly, then righted itself. Rebecca handed me the bag of clothes and I shuffled into the bathroom alone, closed the toilet lid and sat down. I'd have to get dressed while seated; I wasn't sure how long I could stand up.

Rebecca brought a wheelchair over when I came out. "Ally and Kristi came by yesterday and left cards for you. Do you want to see Brian and your grandma before you leave?"

"Yes."

She kept up the chatter until we reached Brian's room. Tracey sat by his bedside.

"Hey." My voice cracked as Rebecca wheeled me in.

Tracey came over and hugged me.

"I'm happy to see you with your eyes open," she said. "Every time I came into your room, you were asleep." She pulled back her chair, so I could sit next to Brian.

"Hi sleepyhead," Brian said as he squeezed my hand.

"Good to see you too," I said. My lingering fear for his health lifted. He would recover. He looked like the same old Brian. I glanced over his injuries. He sported a few cuts on his face as well.

Tracey sat by his feet as we talked. "See, he's as gorgeous as ever."

I mock gagged, but Brian grinned.

"Dad's taking me home today. I guess you guys have to stay a few more days."

Brian gave me a sympathetic look—he knew I dreaded being home alone with Dad. "I wish they would release me. I'm sick of being in this bed." With his left leg encased in a black boot, he wasn't going anywhere soon.

"At least it's your left leg. You can still drive," I said. "How're you feeling?"

"Like I was run over."

"Not quite, but almost." I grimaced. "My whole body hurts. Did you see Grandma?"

"Yeah, she's okay, a little banged up like we are. She insisted the nurse wheel her into each of our rooms, so she could see us. Bet they loved being bossed around." He chuckled.

"I slept through several visits." It bothered me. I considered throwing myself from the wheelchair, so I could extend my stay.

Too late. Dad walked in.

"Hey kids," he said. He stood there awkwardly. "Jess, you ready to go?"

"Can I see Grandma first?"

"I just passed them wheeling her down to x-ray. You can visit her tomorrow."

"Okay." I wanted to cling to Grandma like a life preserver.

He looked at Brian. "I'm going to take Jessie home and get her settled. I'll come back later to check on you and Mom. Rebecca, can you wheel Jessie down to the pickup area in the parking garage? I'll bring the car around to pick you both up."

"No problem," said Rebecca.

"He'll be on his best behavior with all this going on," Brian leaned close and whispered.

He'd read my mind. "Yeah, let's hope." I attempted a smile. I didn't want him to worry since I worried enough for the two of us. Impending doom, here I come. He would drop the act he put on for Mom with only me at home. His true self would emerge, with free reign.

CHAPTER 35

JESSIE

The ride home was quiet. I didn't exhale until we pulled into the driveway.

"Here's a twenty. Why don't you call Mariano's and order pizza for dinner since I have to go back to the hospital?" Dad said.

"Okay, thanks." He must have cheered up. Usually, he would let me fend for myself.

"Thanks for the ride, Mr. Taylor," Rebecca said.

We walked into the house. She sat in the kitchen and I went to put my bag in my room. Baby followed me everywhere, her little tail in overdrive. I scooped her up.

"Did you miss me?" She kept trying to lick my face, but I held my chin up so she couldn't reach it. "You're the best baby, aren't you?" I walked back into the kitchen.

"Do you want to stay for pizza?" I asked Rebecca.

"Do you want me to stay? I have homework I need to finish, but I could go get it and come back." She reached out to pet Baby.

"No, I'm okay. I'll probably eat and then fall asleep again," I said.

"Are you sure?"

"Yes, I'm fine."

She pursed her lips. "Okay, I guess. Text me if you need anything."

"Will do," I said.

After she left, I rummaged around the kitchen drawers to find a coupon for Mariano's. My stomach grumbled just thinking about its salty, cheesy deliciousness. Thirty minutes later, I happily settled myself on the couch with the pizza box on my lap, the TV remote within easy reach and the TV tuned to *Girls*. I opened the pizza box and inhaled. It didn't get any better than this. I turned the volume up on the TV and thought, how do you like that, Dad?

By the time the episode ended, I'd eaten half of the pizza. With a full tummy, I relaxed completely. I put the pizza box aside and got comfortable on the couch. If I heard Dad pull up, I would run the box into the kitchen.

Hours later, I blinked at the flickering light from the TV. I sat up and looked at my phone. It read eleven pm and Dad wasn't home yet. It didn't surprise me, but it was dumb of me to fall asleep on the couch where he would see me as soon as his drunk ass came home. The quiet house made me uneasy. I needed to be awake and ready to run just in case.

Silently, I paced the empty house, checking the driveway often for his car. I always trusted my gut. Baby, tired of following me, settled on the couch and just watched.

I didn't want to be caught in my room if he came home drunk. My bedroom didn't have an exit path. I stood by the living room window and stretched. My body ached, and my head felt like a heavy, painful boulder on my shoulders.

After an hour or so, I went to the family room and sat by the sliding glass doors. A bookshelf would hide me from a casual glance into the room. Dad didn't usually hang out in this room after a bender. He preferred the bigger TV in the living room. The wall in the family room was cool as I sat back against it, and a cold draft swirled in from the sliding glass doors. Baby found me and snuggled beside me. I assumed Dad had fallen off the wagon. With no one to witness or stop his actions, I was expecting the worst.

I hoped he would think I was over at Rebecca's house. My eyelids blinked slowly, and my head nodded down toward my chest. Sometime later, my eyes snapped wide when I heard the front door creak. My phone indicated it was 1 am. I put my hand on Baby, so she wouldn't run to the door. I smelled fried food and heard the crinkle of what I assumed to be a fast food bag. My heart pounded in my chest. Baby shivered under my hand.

"Jessie?" I heard Dad bellow my name as he opened my bedroom door. I could hear him stumbling around, knocking things over in my room.

"I told her to stay home. I should go over to Rebecca's and pick her up right now," he said loudly to himself.

Clever idea, go over to Rebecca's house, you big drunk. While muttering threats, he pulled the food from the bag and settled on the couch to eat. The TV clicked on and my heart started to slow. Based on experience, he would eat and then pass out. My butt grew numb waiting for the blessed event. Finally, he began to snore. I pulled a blanket off the couch and curled up by the family room wall. I couldn't take the chance of sleeping on the couch or in my bedroom. If he got up in the middle of the night, I wasn't sure how he would react. Baby, of course, stayed glued to my side. I kissed her small, smooth head.

As I lay on the drafty floor, I thought about a WWII movie I'd watched with Brian. I could relate to the soldiers, enduring cold and hunger while they waited. The exhausted resignation on their faces, the knowledge they would have to stay alert to remain alive. At least I wasn't in a foxhole in the dead of winter. The thought brought a childhood memory to mind. Brian and I, with a bunch of friends, dug a deep foxhole in the woods as part of our war games. A Lord of the Flies mentality reigned in the woods near our home. With no adult supervision, we acted like crazy people. We would set traps on the ground for each other, jump from trees and chase each other endlessly. The memory made me smile as I surrendered to exhaustion.

In the morning, while Dad still snored, I crept past him to get ready for school. I could smell whiskey on him from five feet away. I wrote him a note telling him I would see him after school. One good thing, he wouldn't remember his drunken search for me the night before. As I put the note on the counter, I noticed a card addressed to me in our pile of mail. It wasn't marked with postage, so it must have been hand delivered. I recognized Alex's black, boxy handwriting. The card featured a golden retriever puppy wishing me well. Inside, he hadn't signed his name, but had sketched a beautiful red Cardinal. I shoved the card into my backpack as my eyes burned with tears. Great, just what I needed.

On the bus, I handed the card to Rebecca. "Look what was in the mail."

She opened it and looked at the drawing. "Pretty, but it's so not cool of him to keep contacting you." She handed it back.

"I know. It's bad enough without being reminded of him," I said.

We arrived at school and I shuffled to our usual spot like a tired zombie. Of course, Alex stared at me from across the hall. I met his sad gaze. As I lowered my eyes, I wondered if I shared his expression.

Large black tennis shoes appeared next to mine. Looking up, I saw Will. My heart lifted, and I smiled. My reaction to him surprised me every time.

"Hey, it's so good to see you. How're you feeling?" He enveloped me in a warm embrace. He felt so good.

"I'm okay…a little tired and sore, but it'll go away soon," I said.

He kept one arm around my shoulders. "I stopped by the hospital to see you, but they wouldn't let me in since I wasn't family," he said.

"Oh, that stinks." I looked at Rebecca. "How did you get in?"

"I lied and said I was your sister." She shrugged and smirked.

"I don't know if you're aware, but Rebecca will rule the world some-day," I said to Will.

"She's obviously clever." The bell rang indicating it was time to go to class. "Let me know if I can help in anyway. I mean it. Okay?" He stared into my eyes.

"Okay."

"See you later." He hugged me again before he walked away.

I chanced a look at Alex to see his reaction. If looks could kill, Will would have been dead. I hoped it hurt Alex to see Will and me together. He deserved a big old swig of his own medicine.

"Wow, Will likes you a lot," Rebecca said as we walked upstairs.

"Seems like it. I feel so guilty about it. I kissed him at the party and then told him I needed time to get over Alex."

"You were honest with him. That's good," she said.

I shrugged and we split off toward our separate lockers. My next major concern involved avoiding Mrs. Palmer.

It turned out to be easy. My head hurt so badly by my free period that I went to Mrs. Powell, the nurse. I knocked lightly on her open office door. She looked up from her desk and waved me in.

"Jessie, how are you feeling? I heard about the car accident." I watched her eyes move over my face. Small cuts still dotted my cheeks.

"I'm okay, but I wondered if I could lie down? It's my free period and my head is killing me."

"Of course. Let me get you a glass of water too. Make sure you drink enough water, so your body can recover." She led me back to the small room with a cot and blanket. "I'll wake you up in thirty minutes or so."

A pro—and con—of attending a small Christian school was that everyone knew everything. I laid my heavy, bumpy head down and gratefully fell asleep.

"Honey, it's time to wake up." The nurse gently shook my shoulder. I clawed my way out of a dark pit to get to consciousness.

I mumbled okay and struggled to sit up. As I rubbed my face, the nurse handed me another glass of water.

"Drink this. It may help you feel better," she said.

I took the plastic cup and gladly drained it. The water did help. "Thank you."

Getting so little sleep last night certainly wasn't helping my head.

"Oh and Mrs. Palmer came by while you were lying down. She asked me to tell you to stop by her office after school today."

"Okay." Shit. I went into the staff bathroom, washed my hands and briefly looked at my face. I didn't wear a lot of make-up, just mascara and eyeliner, but what I had on still seemed fine. I looked so pale. As I came out of the bathroom, I overheard Mrs. Powell talking to Mr. Disher, our principal.

"How's Jessie feeling?" he asked.

"Her head hurts, of course and she's tired. I worry about her. She seems so fragile," said Mrs. Powell.

Her comment made me bristle. She had that wrong—I wasn't fragile. Something within me was hard like steel and utterly emotionless. I understood the term 'killer instinct' perfectly. I hoisted my backpack onto my shoulder and made my way to class.

At the end of the day, my plan to hurry to the bus so I could avoid Mrs. Palmer failed. She must have read my mind because she was waiting for me by my locker.

She smiled as I neared. "Hey, how are you?"

"Okay," I said, staring over her shoulder.

"Could you come to my office for a few minutes? I wanted to speak with you."

With a direct request, I could only agree. I followed her to her office.

"Have a seat," she said.

With dread, I sat down.

"I'm sorry to hear you and your family were in a car accident. I hope your mom and Brian are doing well?"

"They're okay. Brian will be discharged in a day or two and my mom will hopefully be discharged by the end of the week."

"Good. I'm glad to hear it." She paused and took a sip of water. "I wanted to talk with you about your argument with Amanda last week. Do you remember our talk?"

"Yes." I hoped she believed my bluff.

"You do remember?"

"Yes," I answered again. She stared at me and said nothing for a moment. I could tell she didn't believe me.

"I have some concerns based on our conversation. With your best interests in mind, I'm going to take further action to contact your parents, since they haven't returned my calls."

My stomach hit the floor. I had prayed this wouldn't happen.

"I wanted to let you know," she watched my face for a reaction.

"Can I be excused, please?" I needed to escape.

"I'm only doing this to help you. I realize it doesn't appear that way."

"Fine." Halfway to the door, I turned back to her.

"Telling them won't help me. It'll get me killed," I said. I hurried away from her office.

Doomed. I might as well give up. I didn't even remember getting on the bus. The bus dropped me off; Dad's car was parked in the driveway. I dejectedly walked into the house. Everything was in place. Where was the psycho?

"Jessie?" he called out to me as he walked down the hallway.

"Hi Dad."

"We're leaving for the hospital." He pointed his finger at me. "Before we get there, don't even think of telling your mother I went out last night, it will only worry her, and I only played cards with some buddies."

He grabbed my shoulder and dug his fingers into my skin. "Do you understand me?"

"Yes, I won't say anything." I cringed away from him. Yeah, right. I would tell her as soon as I got the chance.

We rode to the hospital in an uncomfortable silence. If only looks could kill. I stared hatefully at his back as we made our way to Mom's room. I stopped a gasp from leaving my lips. Mom was pale, with cuts and a large bruise on the left side of her face. My eyes welled with tears. I went to her right side and held her hand.

"It's so good to see you. I was worried about you." She reached out her hand and caressed my face.

I swallowed hard. Her voice sounded soft and weak. Dad, on the left side of the bed, bent forward and kissed her cheek.

"How do you feel?" I studied her face.

Dad fussed with Mom's blankets and pulled them higher. He took her left hand in his and rubbed it gently. He never took his eyes off her face.

"I'm better; don't worry. The doctor thinks I could be released in a few more days."

"That's good, if they think you're ready." From the looks of her, I didn't agree.

"Before you visit Grandma, I wanted to tell you she's developed pneumonia. She's under a tent to help her breathe. Don't be scared. You know how tough she is." Mom attempted a smile.

"That's awful. How did she get pneumonia?" I asked.

"They don't really know, sweetie. She's older and her immune system may be weaker."

I shook my head. Things got worse and worse.

Dad cleared his throat; he wanted all of Mom's attention.

"I'll go check on Brian and Grandma," I said.

"That's a good idea." He pulled his chair closer to Mom's bed.

"I'll be back in a bit. Can I bring you anything?"

"No, sweetie," Mom said as she gazed at me.

Grandma's room was at the opposite end of the floor. The door was ajar; I peeked my head around it. Grandma slept peacefully under the hum of the plastic tent. I crept over to her bed. The sound of the machines and blinking lights filled her room. Her chest rose and fell evenly. Crying, I left before I disturbed her. I stood outside and tried to pull myself together. Wiping my tears, I went to see Brian.

"Hey," I said. He was staring at the TV.

"Hey, what's wrong? You've been crying."

"Yeah, I just saw Grandma. If something happens to her, I don't think I can take it."

"Come on, she'll be fine. You know she's strong."

"Okay," I mumbled. "Are they releasing you soon?

"I hope so, I'm ready to get out of here. I'm so bored. The doctor said he may discharge me tomorrow."

"That's good," I said, but it wasn't good. The worst scenario played out in my head.

"Have you seen Mom?" I asked.

"Yes, one of the nurses wheeled me to her room. She looks worse than Grandma."

"They both look awful to me." I grimaced. "Do you think Grandma is in serious condition?"

"The nurse said she's in stable condition. She'll be okay," he said.

My brow creased with worry. I decided not to tell him Dad had come home drunk last night.

"How was your night with Dad?" Brian asked.

"Fine. I stayed in my room." I stared at the TV and pretended nonchalance. Unlike our parents, I found it hard to lie to him. I didn't know what to do about another evening at home with Dad. I couldn't go to

Rebecca's; it was a school night. I knew he would drink every night until Mom came home.

The thing I dreaded most played out in my mind; I would hide from Dad, but Brian wouldn't. With Brian's injuries, Dad could seriously hurt him. My mind reeled with the possibilities.

We talked and watched TV for fifteen minutes, my anxiety rising all the while. Finally, I couldn't sit still a moment longer.

"I'm going to see Grandma," I lied again.

I walked a circuit of the hospital floor, trying to figure out how to prevent Brian and I from being home alone with Dad. What the hell could I do? On my second circuit of the floor, I noticed Dad entering Brian's room. Inspiration struck—or desperation, more like. I hurried to Mom's room. She beamed when she saw me and reached out her hand. I took it and sat down.

"Dad didn't come home last night until one a.m. and he was drunk," I said in a rush. "I hid from him all night and he doesn't even remember."

"What?" She shook her head.

"You have to come home tomorrow. Brian and I can't be left alone with him. He's drinking again," I said.

"How do you know he drank?" I could see in her face she didn't want to believe me.

"What else would he be doing until one a.m.? He passed out on the couch and he reeked of booze." I searched her face.

Mom took a deep breath, and my brief hope crashed. She would do nothing. If she didn't see it, she could ignore it.

"Are you trying to get Dad in trouble? He's been doing really well," she said.

Fury flooded my brain. Of course, it was my problem. I hated her. She was as bad as him. I jerked my hand away.

"Whatever, Mom, never mind. When one of us is dead, you'll believe me." My jaw clenched, and I turned to glare out the window.

Dad walked back into the room a few minutes later. I scooted my chair away, staring out the window or watching TV while Dad talked to her.

It didn't seem long before his chair scraped against the floor. "Well, we better go. Visiting hours are over." He gave Mom a kiss and hug.

If she said goodbye to me, I didn't hear her.

My anger continued to stew as we drove home. We pulled into the driveway, but Dad left the car running.

"I have a couple of errands to run," he said.

"Okay." I pretended to be clueless. Before I reached the front door, he sped away. I went into the kitchen and took a couple of pain relievers. My head throbbed. The leftover pizza from last night would be fine for dinner. I turned on the oven. Microwaved pizza was gross.

I set up my little kingdom of pizza, the couch and the remote. It was awesome to eat in peace. And I could turn up the TV as loud as I wanted. I watched episodes of *American Horror Story* on demand. The show didn't scare me. I had experienced true horror. Instead of falling asleep on the couch, I got up, threw away the pizza box and changed into my white nightgown. I grabbed my sleeping bag from my bedroom closet and headed to the family room, assuming the same spot from the night before. Then I sat for a while, legs crossed, and read my Biology chapters.

CHAPTER 36

LENA

Wake up! He's coming.

The family room was completely dark. I sat up and kicked the sleeping bag down to my ankles. My gut swirled. The shit was going hit the fan. My eyes rested on the heavy, ornate candlestick on the fireplace mantel. I picked it up and felt the weight in my hand. Heavy enough to bash his skull in; it would work. A knife would be good too. I moved toward the kitchen, but before I could get there, the front door slammed open and adrenaline pumped through my body.

"Jessie!" he screamed.

I stood in the entrance to the family room. The dumb shit didn't notice me and stomped to Jessie's room. I rolled my neck side to side to loosen it, spread my legs slightly and bent my knees a bit. Joy bubbled inside my body, mixing with the adrenaline like a wonderful cocktail. Party time had arrived. Mom must have called him.

Nice one, Mom. Piss him off so he'll kill us.

"That little bitch," he muttered as he made his way back toward the kitchen. He stopped when he saw me standing silently at the far end of the dining room table. I don't think he noticed the candlestick. He swayed slightly as he tried to stand still.

"You just had to tell her, didn't you? Do you actually think you're going to get rid of me?" He advanced toward me. "You've upset your mother when she's in the hospital." He gritted his teeth and inched closer. His whole body shook. "I hate you. You are worthless. Your little plan isn't going to work because you're out of here."

"You're throwing me out at fifteen? Wow, you're a great dad," I said.

That did it. My comment pushed him over the edge.

He lunged for my throat, hands extended. I swung the candlestick with both hands. It cracked loudly against his hand. He gasped in pain and pulled his hands to his body. He gaped at me with his eyes wide.

I kept the corner of the dining room table between us.

"How'd you like that, Dad? What? Are you confused? Jessie's gone. Now you'll deal with me."

His mouth worked, opening and closing, but no sound emerged. He backed away and gripped the kitchen counter for support.

"Jessie would have died long ago without me. You don't recognize your own creation?" I said, as rage moved through my body. "I am beautiful—don't you agree?"

In shock, he stared at me.

"You think you're pissed?" I yelled. "Your anger is a small flame compared to the inferno I hold within me. How do you like being the receiver of pain instead of the giver? I have to say, giving is more rewarding." I laughed and swung the candlestick at his face.

He cringed away from me.

"What did I say the last time you hit Brian?" With no response from him, I screamed, "WHAT DID I SAY?"

Reining myself in, I said quietly, "I'll remind you. I warned you to never touch us again."

He recovered from his shock and roared back at me in fury and frustration. I threw the candlestick at his head and ran for the front door. The candlestick glanced his right temple.

I was at the front door before he could recover himself. "Do you want to kill me, dickhead? Then you'll have to catch me."

I pushed the door open, jumped the three porch steps and landed lightly on my bare feet. Like a whispering wind, I flowed swiftly over the ground; I could outrun him. His rage and stupidity would make him follow. He wanted to teach me a lesson. Jessie's white nightgown billowed out behind me as I ran. My bare feet tread the road silently. Little rocks dug into the soles of my feet. It was dark, deep into the night. I belonged in the dark; it gave birth to me. The night wrapped itself around me like a comforting cloak. I looked back to see if he was close. Too close. I increased my speed and set my sights on the entrance to the woods. An almost full moon and a few dim porch lights were the only source of illumination. The neighborhood rested peacefully as I ran for our life. The woods were just ahead, with the well-worn dirt path and small hills I could tread with my eyes closed.

Rebecca, Jessie and I, as her shadow, spent countless summers here in imagined worlds. We danced around the woods, caught frogs in the creek and pretended to be princesses, soldiers and fairies, the trees our domain.

I bent slightly and burst through the opening to the woods. My feet hit the soft dirt path and I stumbled over an exposed tree root. Before I could get up, he fell on me. He grasped for my legs as I scrambled to get up. His nails dug into the back of my calf. I kicked at his face and freed myself. I put a comfortable distance between us. His labored breath and unsteady steps let me know he was still plunging forward after me. Moonlight filtered through the trees and provided the only source of light. I slowed a bit so he could continue to follow.

"You'll never catch me," I yelled back, in a sing-song voice. My laughter floated up to the canopy of trees. Confident the sound would push him onward, I taunted, "Here, piggy piggy!" Joy swept through my body and I laughed again.

He panted and muttered between breaths. I clearly heard "her" and "kill." I imagined he would relish choking me like the sweetest dessert. He, however, would not be getting that pleasure. I ran deeper into the woods and farther away from the neighborhood. Surrounded by the thick growth of trees, tall grass, weeds and moss, all sound would be trapped here with us. The foxhole loomed just ahead. Dug wide and deep enough for a 6-foot man to fall into. The grave we dug for him unknowingly. It waited here in the woods for his arrival. We, the children, would survive this war.

The path sloped upward just before the foxhole. I pushed with my back leg as my front leg sailed easily over the opening. Hurdling had prepared us well. I landed clear of the pit and stepped to the left to hide behind a tree. I pulled the nightgown tighter around me, so the white wouldn't show. Still muttering threats, he approached the hole. Gasping in surprise, his foot found air where solid ground had existed a moment before. I stepped out from behind the tree. I watched as his arms pin-wheeled, but gravity and his forward motion carried him down. His hands slid, and his fingers grasped at the dirt wall while he tried to break his fall. His head smacked against a protruding rock with a sickening crunch and he cried out in pain. It sounded like something broke. His neck, I hoped.

I knelt beside the pit. His body lay motionless at the bottom. There were no sounds of breathing. I prayed he could still hear me; his brain would continue to work for a few moments. The smell of dirt and leaves filled my nose. I panted from the run as I leaned over the pit. The smell of whiskey rose from his body.

"I told you. You wouldn't catch me. I'm so happy you're here. I could skip around these woods and shout with glee!"

I lowered my voice and leaned further into the pit. "Some people should not live. Some people only suck the life out of everyone they're near. That's you. You're a parasite and I just scraped you off. You won't be able to suck the life from Jessie and Brian anymore. Your creation led you to your death."

I rose from beside the pit and rubbed my hands together to get off the dirt. His head tilted at an unnatural angle; certainly he was dead. I stepped casually around the pit and then leisurely walked back the way I had come. Everything had gone perfectly.

CHAPTER 37

JESSIE

Startled, I sat up and looked around. Why was I in my bed? I listened to the house. No sounds, no activity and my bedroom door remained shut. Baby slept beside me. Awake now, she peered up at me and wagged her tail. I glanced at my phone. Shit, I'd slept through my alarm.

I put on my fluffy robe, grabbed my phone and slowly opened the door. I looked down at Baby. "Baby, who's here?"

Normally if I said that, she would run around the house and look for Brian, but she stayed. Not that I wanted to see him, but I tentatively called out for Dad.

Nothing. I peeked in my parent's room; the bed hadn't been slept in. Maybe he'd stayed out all night. His car was in the driveway. Shit. Where was he? I grabbed a coat from the closet and went outside. The car was empty. I tiptoed through the dew-soaked grass looking for him. Nothing.

It was already nine am. I looked at my text messages. Rebecca had texted me to ask where I was and if I was okay. I called Brian at the hospital. Thank God, he answered.

"Hey, what's up?" He seemed to be in a good mood.

"I'm still at home. I slept in, but Dad isn't here, and his car is in the driveway."

"He has to be there somewhere if his car is there."

"I've looked in the house and outside. He's not passed out in his car either. What should I do?"

"I don't know, one of his buddies maybe picked him up. When did you see him last?"

"He dropped me off after we visited you and Mom. I haven't seen him since," I said.

"He's supposed to be here in an hour. Hang tight at home and I'll call you if he shows up here. Call me if he shows up at home."

"Okay."

Shit. I would get in trouble for not going to school. I'd blame it on the head trauma. I walked into the bathroom and turned on the shower for the water to warm up. As the spray soaked my head, I glanced at my feet. Light brown water swirled around them. I lifted one foot to take a better look. My toes were muddy, and a long, bloody scratch marked the back of my calf. It stung as the water hit it.

I sank to the floor of the shower. A few scratches marked the palms of my hands as well, like I had caught myself falling. Stepping out, I grabbed a towel from the rack and wrapped it around me. Still dripping water, I went to my room and pulled back the comforter and sheets. At the end of the bed were bits of dirt and blood. The sheet trembled in my hand. I dropped it, but reached for the fitted sheet and pulled them all off the bed. My towel dropped as I walked to the laundry room. I put the sheets in, added detergent and watched as the washer filled with water. When it started agitating, I awoke from my daze. I had mud on my feet, no big deal. It could have happened when I walked around the house this morning, but I knew I hadn't gotten back in bed after my walk, and what about the blood? I lied to myself. I couldn't handle it any other way.

My skin prickled with goosebumps; my hair stood on end. I was two people. The gypsy told the truth. I collapsed in front of the washer.

At some point, I dressed and just sat in front of the TV. The scratch burned on the back of my leg, an unpleasant reminder. Every little sound made me jump. Baby stayed in my lap. After a few hours, I decided to call Brian. He answered after the first ring.

"Hey," he said. "Did Dad show up?"

"No." Numbness spread throughout my body. "He isn't there either?"

"No. I'll tell Mom. They discharged me, and no one is here to pick me up," he said.

"Okay."

"Um, who could pick me up?"

"I'll call Rebecca's mom. She works from home."

"Good idea, thanks."

Rebecca's mom, Rachel, sounded surprised by my call, but happy to help. I rode with her to the hospital to pick up Brian. When we arrived, she went to Brian's room and I went to Mom's. In a way, it felt good to tell her. I had warned her.

Her eyes were closed, but she sat upright as I entered the room. "Hey."

She startled but recovered quickly. "Hi." She paused for a minute and looked at me hopefully. "Did Dad bring you?"

"I haven't seen him since he dropped me off last night. I don't know where he is."

She sighed. "He didn't come home at all?"

"I guess. His car is in the driveway, but I didn't see him. I even looked for him in the yard." She was holding her phone—no doubt she'd been calling him.

"Rebecca's mom is here to pick up Brian. I couldn't think of who else to call," I said.

"Okay." She stared past me.

I wanted to say *I told you so,* but I pressed my lips together to hold back the bitterness.

"Could you have Rebecca's mom come to my room for a minute before she takes you home please?" Mom asked.

"Sure."

I left without another word. At fifteen, I endured my life. Too many things had happened, and I knew more than I ever wanted to.

In Brian's room, Rachel was helping him get situated in the wheelchair.

"My mom wanted to talk to you for a minute, if you don't mind?"

"Oh, okay. I'll go have a chat with her and then we'll head out." She smiled at us. Like her daughter, she operated calmly and efficiently.

Brian waved for me to sit down next to him.

"Do you remember last night?" he said.

No, I didn't remember, but I couldn't tell him. I lied.

"I haven't really thought about it. I woke up in my bed this morning. I remember him dropping me off. I ate leftover pizza for dinner."

"Anything else?" His voice was urgent.

I whispered, "No."

"We don't have much time, if anyone asks you, you ate dinner, watched TV and went to bed. That's it. You didn't hear his car and you weren't aware of him coming home."

"Okay." My heart thumped hard in my chest.

"Look at me. Did you miss any time? Like when you have a thing?" He searched my eyes.

"I don't know," I said.

As we huddled together, Rachel came back.

"All right, let's get the two of you back home." As she studied us, a question crossed her face, but she didn't say anything.

"Hi, I'm Abby, the nurse practitioner, I'm here to help Brian get to the patient pick-up area. Are you ready to go?" She studied the three of us. I was sure Brian noticed her blonde hair and green eyes. "They didn't tell me how handsome you are."

"He sure is," Rachel responded with a smile.

Brian's face turned red and I rolled my eyes. Good Lord, every woman he met flirted with him.

"Since you're here, I'll go ahead and bring the car around," Rachel said.

"Sounds good. We'll be there shortly." She looked around the room and asked, "Do you have everything?"

"Yes, I'm all packed." Our innate politeness helped in all situations.

"Okay, let's get you out of here." She stepped behind Brian's wheel-chair and I followed with his bag. She kept up a cheery patter of conversation as we made our way to the parking garage.

Rachel pulled the car up as we arrived in the pick-up area. She got out and opened the back passenger door.

"Let me help you." Abby said as she wheeled Brian around.

"Thank you, I've got it."

She watched as he maneuvered himself into the car.

"Okay. Take care," she said as she moved the wheelchair back and shut the door.

Finally, we were on our way home. I turned around from the front seat. Brian's face was covered in a sheen of sweat.

"You okay?"

"Yeah, I'm fine." He waved me off.

"What would you guys like for dinner?" Rachel asked as she drove.

"You don't have to get us dinner. I can make something," I said.

Her phone rang. "Hang on a second…hello, yes, we're on our way home…okay. Are you sure? It's no trouble for me to watch after them." She was silent for a minute, then: "Okay, please let me know if I can help out in any way."

She put the phone down and said, "Ted and Alyssa are going to check in on you until your Mom is released. They'll stop by around six."

I thanked God. Sane people would be in charge. Mom didn't count in that category.

Brian and I thanked Rachel and she left us to our own devices for a few hours. We sat on the couch and messed with our phones.

He sat up and nudged my shoulder, then stared at me. "Lena, I need to talk to you."

"What? Did you just call me another name?" I frowned.

He sighed. "No, never mind."

"You call me by another name and I should forget it?"

"Yeah," he grumbled and hobbled off to his room.

CHAPTER 38

DETECTIVE WHEELER

I noted the house numbers as I drove down the street. I loved the neighborhoods with mature trees. Lots of mature trees made a neighborhood, in my opinion. 3120, 3122, 3124, ah, here it was: 3130 Brookhaven Drive. I pulled into the driveway and checked out the house. A nice, red brick ranch with a neatly kept yard. I switched off the ignition and got out.

An older woman answered the door. "May I help you?"

"Hello ma'am, I'm Detective Wheeler from the Stanton Police Department. I'm here regarding Lou's missing person's report."

"Yes. Please come in. I'm Ruth, Lou's mother in law. Can I get you something to drink? Water? Coffee?"

"Coffee would be great if you have it ready, but don't go to any trouble, ma'am" I said. I noted the clean house. Decent furniture, no clutter, and the carpet was recently vacuumed.

"It's no trouble at all." I watched Ruth make the coffee. The lines on her face and silver hair made me guess her age was around seventy, but the spring in her step made her seem younger.

While I waited, I walked into the adjoining family room. Ruth could see me from the kitchen. The mantel drew my eye—two large, ornate candlesticks sat on it. It was lightly coated in dust, but one candlestick had been recently moved. It now sat outside of the dust outline. I took out my notebook and jotted it down.

"Hi, I'm Jan. Lou's wife," said the younger woman who'd walked into the room.

My back faced the hallway, so I hadn't seen her approach. She used a walker to get to her chair.

"Let me help you." I rushed forward to help.

She took my hand as she lowered herself into the dining room chair. "Thank you."

"You're welcome."

Ruth put hot, black coffee in front of me and her daughter. She also laid out spoons, sugar and half 'n' half in a cow figurine. She positioned Jan's walker so she could reach it.

"Thanks, Mom."

"Thank you, Ma'am. It smells wonderful."

Ruth waved the compliment off. Fresh coffee suckered me in every time. I liked her instantly.

"Are you new to the police department, detective? I don't think we've met before," Jan said.

"Yes, I just moved here a few weeks ago from Chicago. I wanted a change of pace." That was a massive understatement.

"Good for you. I'm sure you'll like it here."

I took out my notepad. "When we spoke yesterday you mentioned your husband has been missing for three days?"

"Yes, I called right away—his fellow officers came by the hospital and said they would find him, but they haven't yet. And when I filed the missing person's report, they said it isn't a crime for an adult to be missing without an indication of foul play."

"Yes Ma'am, that's correct," I said.

"I had to report him missing. Something's wrong. He would never be gone for this long. He's never not come home. Not one night of our marriage." Her eyes welled with tears. "His car is in the driveway, but he hasn't been home. The kids and I were in a car accident last week, so at the time only Jessie, my daughter, was here. My son and I were still in the hospital."

"Sorry to hear that. I hope you and your family are recovering."

"We'll be fine once my husband is home. I'm worried to death. I've called every hospital in the area too," she said, exasperated.

"I understand. Why don't we go over some basics first? Could you confirm your husband's height, weight, hair color…?"

"Of course, Lou is six feet tall, about two hundred pounds and he's mostly bald so he shaves his head."

"You may have checked this, but did your husband call himself off at work?"

"No. I called the Chief the next day and he hadn't heard from him. I asked him to call me if Lou contacted him." She stared at her lap and appeared to be embarrassed.

"My husband recently completed rehab for alcohol addiction, so I thought he might be drinking again. Maybe he's holed up somewhere drinking or is embarrassed to come home." She looked at me hopefully. "That happens, right?"

"It's possible." It was always hard to talk with the wife. Especially when it sounded like her husband had taken off. "Did he leave his wallet in the car? Is there any indication he came into the house? For example, were the car keys in the house?" I asked.

"No car keys or wallet in the car or the house. The clothes he wore that day aren't here either," she said.

"Has there been any activity on his bank cards?"

"No."

"Do you mind if I speak with your daughter now?"

"That's fine, but she doesn't know anything." She leaned toward me. "Why aren't they searching for my husband? He's one of them. I just don't understand the delay."

"We have been. The last known sighting of him was at Charley's around twelve-thirty a.m. Wednesday."

"Oh." She hung her head.

"I need to interview Jessie to see if she can offer us anymore information." I stretched my hand out to gently grasp hers. "I would like to speak to her in private if you don't mind." I smiled reassuringly.

She raised her voice and called for her daughter. A moment later Jessie walked into the dining room. She was taller than average, around five-seven... a pretty slender girl with big, dark eyes and dark hair. She eyed me cautiously. In fact, her whole demeanor seemed watchful. She sat in the dining room chair closest to the door. I wondered if she did that on purpose.

"Hi Jessie, I'm Detective Wheeler. I know this must be a very hard time for you, but I need to speak with you about the last time you saw your father," I said.

Most teenagers wouldn't maintain eye contact, but Jessie did. She assessed me.

She nodded.

"Can you tell me about the last time you saw your father?"

She took a deep breath. "We went to the hospital after I got home from school and stayed until visiting hours were over. Dad dropped me off here and said he had some errands to run. I ate leftover pizza, did my homework, watched TV and went to bed around 10 pm. He hadn't come home by the time I went to bed."

Clearly a rehearsed answer.

"Did he call you to say he would be coming home late?" I said.

"No."

"Did you hear him come home during the night?" I said.

"No, I sleep with a fan. It drowns out noise."

Something in her tone made me question her answer. In the not-so-distant past, I had been a detective in a much larger city. I'd learned to trust my gut.

"Did your Dad appear to be stressed or worried?"

"No. Mostly he looked forward to going out." Her face remained impassive as she answered.

"Why would you say that?" I said.

"He couldn't wait to drop me off at home. He sped away as soon as I got out of the car." She shrugged.

"Any ideas on where he wanted to go?" I said.

"He said to run errands, but I'm pretty sure he went to drink somewhere. He came home drunk the night before he disappeared," she said.

"Does your mom know he drank the evening before his disappearance?"

"I told her." She cleared her throat. Emotionally this kid appeared locked down. No indication of sadness or distress on her face.

"I apologize, but may I use your restroom?" I said.

"Sure, it's down the hall on the right. It's all pink, you can't miss it." She smirked.

On a hunch, I made my way toward the bathroom, but quickly walked past it. The first room on the left must have been Jessie's. Makeup and perfume littered the dresser. I stepped in and looked around. I didn't see a fan; she'd lied to me. I quickly left her room and went into the bathroom. Wow, she wasn't kidding about the pink. I had never seen pink plush carpeting in a bathroom.

My father drank excessively too, so I could relate to Jessie's detachment. I distanced myself from my father as soon as I could. When Jan called in to report Lou missing I asked around the station. His peers were quiet about him. He didn't appear to be well liked in the department, but me being new to the station, I thought maybe they didn't want to talk to me about it. His fellow officers were called to his home two years ago for a domestic disturbance. I had heard he had a drinking problem.

I walked back into the dining room. A boy, I assumed her brother, was talking with Jessie at the table.

"Hi, I'm Detective Wheeler." I reached out to shake his hand.

He stood and grasped my hand. "I'm Brian, Jessie's brother."

Down south, in Georgia, where I grew up, we called boys like Brian *a big 'ole hunk of boy.* "Are you both in high school?" I said.

"Yeah, I'm a senior and Jessie's a freshman." He turned toward his sister in a protective position. They both watched me carefully. I could see they were similar in their caution. Brian's eyes assessed me as well.

"I have enough information for now, but if you think of any detail that would be relevant, please give me a call," I said.

"Okay." Brian answered instead of Jessie.

I said to Jessie, "I bet you're missing your Dad a bunch."

"No." She answered with a snort. My question was ridiculous to her.

"Jess!" Brian frowned. "I can't believe you said that. Of course we miss Dad."

She narrowed her eyes at me. She recognized the setup. For a second, a look moved over her face like a shadow. It felt like a warning. A chill ran through my body.

Jan came back into the dining room.

"Are you done?" She looked at Brian and Jessie and then back to me.

"Yes," I said.

She nodded and slowly took her seat again.

"We need to talk about setting up a search," she said.

The hardest part of the job required my honesty. "I'm not sure if the police force will conduct a further search. It's not illegal to be missing as an adult. I don't see any indications of foul play at this point. He may have left of his own free will," I said as gently as I could.

"No. Something is wrong. I know he wouldn't voluntarily leave me," she said.

"I will discuss a search with the police chief, but if he doesn't agree to one, you could always organize your own search. I'm sorry, ma'am. If he were a child or if we suspected foul play, it would be a different story."

Ruth walked in.

"Mom, the police won't do a search if they don't suspect foul play." Her face crumpled in grief. Ruth stood behind her daughter and put her hands on her shoulders.

"Is that police procedure, Detective Wheeler?" She watched me expectantly.

"Yes ma'am," I said.

"He said we could organize our own search," Jan pleaded to her mother.

"Well then, that's what we'll do." Ruth patted her daughter's shoulder, and Jan relaxed visibly.

I gathered my notes and put them back into the vanilla folder. "That's it for now. I'll be in touch about next steps."

"Thank you, we appreciate your help." She walked me to the door.

"You're welcome," I said.

The interview had sparked my interest even more. The kids were involved somehow. I got back in my unmarked car and put the folder beside me in the passenger seat. My next stop, the other bars in Stanton.

CHAPTER 39

BRIAN

I couldn't believe Jessie just said that to the cop. The cop got it too. Anyone could see that she didn't care about Dad. What the hell was I going to do with her? With Dad missing, I couldn't tell Grandma about Jessie. What if the detective decided to talk to her again? I had to figure out a way to make Lena show up. I had to know what happened. Even thinking about it seemed surreal. My sister possessed a second, distinct personality who acted out of her own accord.

The hair stood up on the back of my neck. I sat on the couch and stared numbly at the TV.

"BRIAN!" Grandma yelled to get my attention.

"Sorry, Gran, I zoned out."

"I can tell. I'm taking your mom for a hip therapy session. We'll be back in two hours or so," she said.

"Okay."

With Mom and Grandma out of the house, I had to talk to Lena now. An idea came to me. When we were younger, I would hold Jessie down and tap on her head. I pretended to spit on her as well. It made her crazy. Which, of course, is why I did it.

I got up, hobbled over to the window, and watched the car pull out of the driveway. How could I do this with the cast on my leg? I didn't want to hurt myself. Even with my strength, I didn't know if I could hold Lena down.

I needed to know if Lena had done something to Dad.

"Hey Jess, c'mere," I yelled to her from the living room. I sat down on the floor with plenty of space around me.

"Why?" she yelled back from her bedroom.

"My leg hurts. Get me a pain pill and some water?"

"Oh, sure."

I knew that would get a response.

A few minutes later she walked into the living room. "Here you go." She sat down next to me and handed me a pill and a glass of water.

"Thanks." I swallowed it with a gulp of water.

"Why are you on the floor? Wouldn't you be more comfortable on the couch?" she said.

"Yeah, probably." I leaned over and bumped my shoulder into hers. "Remember when I use to hold you down and pretend to spit on you?"

"Unfortunately, yes. You're an idiot," she said.

"Think I could pin you down now?" I pushed with my good leg and tipped her over. Before she could react, I trapped her arms under me with our combined weight.

"Get off. You're crushing me, moron," she grunted.

"Nope, I want to tap your head and see if that still makes you crazy." I tapped on her forehead. "Hello, anyone in there?"

She wiggled relentlessly under my weight. My good leg pushed behind her legs so she couldn't kick me.

"Get off. I can't breathe," she gasped.

I blew air in her ear. She screamed and kicked her legs. "Hello, anyone in there." When we were kids we called this the torture test.

"Brian, stop!"

"You're talking so you must be getting air." I tapped on the side of her head and said, "HELLOOO, anyone there?" I sweated profusely trying to hold her down. I laughed…I had forgotten how fun this was. The next second, my breath left my body as something hit my balls, hard.

She stood and kicked me in the stomach before I could catch my breath, then brought her foot back for another kick.

"Lena, stop!" I yelled. "I need to talk to you."

Her foot hesitated. I scrambled to sit up and fought the urge to vomit. Oh shit, I may be sterile.

I studied her hard face and black eyes. Yes, this was Lena.

"What's wrong with you? I don't appreciate being annoyed," she said.

I held my hands up in the universal gesture of surrender. "Sorry, I needed to talk to you. I thought if I made Jessie mad, you would come."

"You're correct. The only thing keeping me from kicking you in the guts again is her affection for you. What do you want?"

"Dad's missing. Do you know what happened?" I asked.

Her eyes narrowed in response. "You don't want me to answer that question. Knowing is a burden," she said.

I bowed my head and pushed my hair off my sweaty forehead with a trembling hand. Maybe I didn't want or need to know. I shook my head. Resignation settled over me.

"I have to know to protect Jessie," I said.

"Fine. Dad, as you call him, is dead."

Black dots appeared in my peripheral vision. More black dots followed, narrowing my vision to a small circle. My body broke out in a full, cold sweat.

"Brian!" She nudged my knee with her foot. The black dots receded.

"How did he die?" I said.

"Everything came together perfectly so it could happen." She knelt in front of me, her eyes sparkling with joy. "Only he and I were in the house. He showed up drunk and pissed because Jessie told Mom he'd been drinking the night before. He came home and tried to kill us."

"How did he try to kill you?" I asked.

"He lunged for my throat, but I anticipated what he would do. You know the candlestick from our mantel?"

"Yeah," I said.

"When he lunged, I swung the candlestick and hit his hand. It definitely broke a finger or two. He tried for me again, but I threw the candlestick at his head and ran for the front door."

"Oh my God," I could only mumble.

"I told him if he wanted to kill me he would need to catch me. I called him an asshole or something. Anyway, I knew the dumbass would chase me," she said.

Her dark eyes gleamed with delight. Killing him had been unbelievably fun for her.

"I ran for the woods, and in a flash of genius, I remembered the foxhole. I knew he would fall into it. I knew the fall would kill him. You know when you just know something?" She clenched her fists and leaned close to me.

"Yeah, I know," I said, surprised I could answer.

"So, I ran to the foxhole. I jumped over it. He fell in. He chased me to his own death. Destiny decided it." She beamed.

"Have you been back?" I tried not to imagine my father in the pit, but the image came anyway. His broken body lying there in the dirt.

"No, why would I go back?" she asked.

"To see if he's there."

"He's dead. I'm sure of it. You can't go there either. Let the police or someone else find him."

"What did you do with the candlestick?" I said.

"When I came back to the house, I picked it up and put it back on the mantle. It didn't have blood on it or anything."

"We have to clean it in case they decide to dust for prints or something." My stomach rolled in anxiety.

"You can clean it," she said. She studied me with those cold dark eyes.

I guessed what would happen now. It would look odd, of course, but would probably still be determined an accident. I prayed no evidence of Jessie existed near the hole or in the woods. I couldn't risk going to the pit myself. It might attract attention.

CHAPTER 40

BRIAN

One week had passed and still no Dad. The police didn't have any definitive information. The last known sighting of Dad entailed him leaving a bar in downtown Stanton. The police hadn't bothered to search the house. They thought he'd deserted us.

I sat on the couch with the windows open and enjoyed the warm spring breeze that blew through. Grandma had opened every window in the house to air it out. I could hear Jessie and Rebecca outside laughing as they tried to skateboard over a ramp. I grinned every time I heard her laugh. I watched her closely as much as I could. Happy best described her. She never mentioned Dad and appeared not to worry about him coming back. I wondered if at some level, she knew.

"Here you go, sweetie," Grandma said as she brought me my lunch, grilled cheese and potato chips. The smell of the hot melted cheese and butter made my mouth water. Grandma ruled!

"Thanks."

She moved in after Dad went missing. Mom couldn't cope with the simplest of things, and Grandma took over with a vengeance. She hired contractors to paint the inside of the house a pale yellow. Her next step entailed ripping out all the cabinets and countertops. I don't think Mom noticed.

I shifted my leg cast and balanced my lunch on my lap. Another two weeks and I could stop wearing the boot. As I sat there, I could hear the leaves on the trees softly rustling together and the birds singing.

Grandma came in and watched Jessie and Rebecca from the window. She put her hands over her eyes as Jessie flew off the ramp with her skateboard. She landed hard and fell off the board.

"Shit," she said as she picked up her board to try again.

"Jessica Ruth Taylor!" Grandma admonished her from the open window.

Jessie grinned impishly at her, "Oops, sorry, Grandma."

Grandma clutched her hands to her chest.

"I hope she doesn't break her leg."

"She won't," I said.

Jessie possessed all kinds of hidden skills. Grandma went back into the kitchen to do who knew what. She moved constantly.

My notepad fell beside my leg as I ate. I bent to pick it up. Scanning the list, I noted a couple more of the guys and then put the notepad aside. The list consisted of volunteers who'd signed up to look for signs of Dad in a two-mile radius from the house. I made sure the neighbors would be the group to search the woods. I hated picking any group to find Dad, but the adults would hopefully handle it the best. They might not even find him.

Jessie and Grandma would go with another group in the opposite direction. Mom and I would stay at home due to our injuries.

The search would begin the next morning at ten. The thought made my stomach turn over. It was the day that would determine our future.

CHAPTER 41

DETECTIVE WHEELER

The flyer with Lou Taylor's face and description lay on top of my case files. I picked up the flyer, read it again and put it back down. I rose from my desk and walked over to the water cooler. My tour of the downtown bars had drawn a vivid picture of Lou Taylor. The man who'd spent thirty days away during rehab, only to return to the bars as soon as he was home.

The curious thing about my bar tour— it didn't provide a person who left with Lou or anyone who would have given him a ride. Based on my observations, Lou didn't really have any close friends in either the bar crowd or the police station.

I walked back to my desk, took a sip of water and looked at the flyer again. The bank reported no activity on his cards, along with no communication with his family. The prospects for a good outcome were slim.

Even when people disappeared willingly, there was always some kind of money trail. I didn't have high hopes the search would result in any good news.

I kicked off my loafers under my desk and reached for my hiking boots. The sturdy brown boots hadn't seen much action. It would be good to get out and stretch my legs. I had spent too much time at my desk lately.

By ten it looked to be a beautiful spring day. The sun shone in a clear blue sky. I arrived at the Taylor home along with what looked to be fifty other volunteers. Several other officers were also involved in the search. I walked up the driveway toward Brian who stood in the middle of the crowd with his boot and cast still in place on his broken leg.

"Okay, there are five groups. Each group will take a direction and the ten of you will fan out. If you could go about two miles in your direction, that will be our first search grid," he shouted to the crowd.

Organized kid. He was mature for a seventeen-year-old boy. I maneuvered over to him through the crowd.

"Hey Brian, how are you?" I held out my hand.

"Detective, I'm okay. How're you?"

"I'm good. I wanted to come out and help with the search."

"Thank you." He frowned at his list. "Since you wore boots, why don't you join group two? It's mostly made up of people from our neighborhood, but their search will spread to the woods."

"Sounds fine. You've done an excellent job putting this together. Is your sister here as well?"

"Yes, she's over there." He nodded in her direction.

I looked and saw Jessie talking with a tall blond boy and a dark-haired girl. It was good she had friends with her today. She noticed me and squinted her eyes. I gave her a nod and she returned it.

Brian's voice boomed over the crowd. "Okay, everybody get with your group. Nominate a group leader and start in your assigned direction."

I noticed Ruth in Jessie's group as well. My group gathered in the neighbor's driveway, so I headed that direction.

"Hi, I'm Ted. We live just a few doors down," he said.

We shook hands. "I'm Detective Wheeler from the Stanton Police Department."

"Oh, maybe we should make you the leader then?"

"No, I'm sure you'll do fine. I'm just here to help."

He clapped his hands together and told everyone to fan out in a vertical line and stay in formation, so we would ensure we thoroughly searched our part of the grid. We started out, but it was a little awkward as some of us were in the middle of the road. I walked where the road met the grass.

After a week, I didn't think we'd find much, but you never knew. We'd only walked about a quarter mile before we entered the woods. An easily identifiable dirt path wound its way in between the growth of trees. I hiked along, stopping at times to look under dried branches and leaves. Nothing out of the ordinary so far. If we found something, we were supposed to call out, so we could mark the spot. With me along, at least they wouldn't need to call the police if anything came up. I pulled out my bandana and wiped the sweat from my forehead. Ted kept track of the distance, but I guessed we'd walked a little over a mile into the woods. I stuffed my bandana in my back pocket and started forward. I noticed it then—a heavy, putrid smell.

Once you've smelled a rotting body, you don't forget it. I scanned the ground up ahead more closely but didn't see anything obvious.

"Ted?" I called out.

"Yeah."

"I need everyone in the group to stop." As soon as I said it everyone converged on me.

"Why, what's up?" he asked, but then covered his nose.

"Please, I need all of you to stay back while I look up ahead." The group stared back at me wide-eyed. Some of the women covered their mouths.

"Also, please don't text any messages regarding this discovery until we have more information," I said.

I made my way cautiously forward, led by the smell. Picking up a stick I started to prod the ground in suspicious looking areas. The dirt path led me closer to the smell...and then I saw it. A pit in the ground. A rather large pit; someone had dug this. I moved as close as I wanted to get and stretched my torso to look down.

A dead body lay at the bottom. I inched closer. Tan pants, dark green jacket and loafers. It appeared to be a man. I reached into my pocket for my phone.

"Sue, this is Detective Wheeler. I'm in the woods located at the end of Brookhaven Drive. I've found a body. Please send backup and the coroner to the scene."

I put my phone in my pocket and walked back to the group.

"Was it a dead animal?" Ted asked.

"No, it appears to be a man, but I don't know for sure who. If you don't mind, could you go back to the entrance of the woods and lead the police officers here when they arrive?"

"Sure. What should we do if Jan or Brian see us and the police cars?" Ted said.

"I'll come out and talk with the family when the officers arrive," I said.

"Okay."

Ted and the group walked back toward the entrance to the woods. I fished my bandana out of my pocket and tied it around my head to cover my nose. I moved to the pit and carefully lowered myself into it. It wasn't freshly dug—there was moss and other growth down the sides. With my feet planted on either side of the body, I reached down to feel for a wallet in the back pockets of the pants. Bingo. Carefully, I pulled it free and placed it on the ground next to the pit.

Several rocks protruded at the far end. Once out, I picked up the wallet and moved away to get some fresh air. Opening it, I noticed Lou's picture on the license in the clear pocket. How the hell did he end up in the woods? Could you be so drunk you would wander a mile into the woods? It didn't make sense.

Shit. I wiped my face again and made my way to the tree line. I lead the arriving officers to the scene. I took a deep breath and headed for the house.

CHAPTER 42

JESSIE

Keeping my head down, I stole a sidelong look at Will. I appreciated his presence today. The sun shining on his blond hair made it look like a golden halo. Forgetting myself, I stared openly at him. With his prominent nose and strong chin, his profile looked like that of a Greek god. He must have felt my gaze because he looked over and smiled at me. Every smile sparked joy in my heart. It made no sense to me; I ached for Alex, but I wanted to be with Will as well.

"Would you like some water?" he asked.

"Yeah, thanks." I didn't really, but it would be nice to talk with him for minute. He pulled a bottle out of his backpack and handed it to me.

Cool water soothed my throat. "How're you keeping the water cold?" I said.

"I have a couple of frozen packs with them," he said.

"Good idea." I took another sip. "We should have done the search sooner."

"We aren't done yet and you don't know if the other groups have found anything."

"I know, you're right. I should think positive thoughts. Thanks for helping. I appreciate it." I shielded my eyes as I squinted up at him.

"No problem." He bent his head toward me and said, "I want to help, and I like being around you."

I wrapped my arms around his waist. He put his arms around my shoulders and kissed the top of my head. I desperately needed to be comforted. We stood there for a few minutes holding each other. The volunteers continued walking without us. I stepped back from him.

"I like being around you too," I said.

Will responded with his broad grin. "Let's get together more."

A sound broke into my happy thoughts and my head jerked in the direction of the house.

"Did you hear that?"

"What?" He squinted as he turned in the same direction.

"Someone screamed." I listened carefully and heard it again.

CHAPTER 43

ANNIE

"Mommy?" I whispered. The water bottle dropped from my hand.

"Rebecca?" My head whipped from side to side looking for her.

Rebecca, not far ahead, ran back to me. "What's wrong?"

I grabbed her hand. "Take me home, my mommy screamed."

She frowned and studied my face. "Okay."

"Hurry!" I tugged on her hand.

"Uh, okay. Let's cut through the yards. It will be faster," she said.

I gripped her hand as we walked. Will stayed by me.

I wanted Lena. She kept me safe. I started to run, pulling Rebecca with me.

We all ran, cutting through neighbors' back yards until we reached mine.

"That's my swing set." I pointed it out to Will.

"It's too loud. I don't like this." I covered my ears. Will and Rebecca stared at me open-mouthed. As we rounded the corner of the house, I stopped.

Police cars, their lights flashing, were parked in front of our house. Why were they here? I could hear my mom as I walked up the driveway. And then I saw her. Some man was holding her.

"No, no, no, it can't be him," she said.

The man held her up and another came with a blanket to lay her down. Rebecca's hand held mine tightly.

"Mommy?" I said.

"They said they found a body in the woods. Tell them, Jessie, it can't be Dad. He would never go in the woods." She grabbed a fistful of her own hair and pulled.

As I stood there, a car pulled up and Grandma jumped out and ran toward us.

"What happened?" Grandma looked at the man.

"I'm sorry, ma'am. We believe we found Lou's body in the woods."

Grandma uncoiled Mom's hand from her hair and pulled it to her heart.

My bottom lip trembled. I wanted Brian. Where was my brother?

My eyes found him with a bunch of other people. With my thumb in my mouth, I scooted my butt right next to him, making other people move over.

"I don't like this. I want all these people to go home," I said.

His eyes were red-rimmed. His mouth hung open as he stared at me. He removed my thumb from my mouth.

A lady hugged me. "I'm sorry, Jessie."

I needed to get out of here. I started to run toward Rebecca's house. For a split second, everyone froze in shock, and in the next second everyone rushed toward me. Will grabbed me around the waist and another man stood in front of me with his hands up, ready to block me.

"Hey now, honey, there's nowhere to run." The man stepped closer. He turned his head and yelled, "I need a paramedic."

I wanted Lena. As I fell back in place, someone screamed.

CHAPTER 44

DETECTIVE WHEELER

The coroner's office wasn't far from the police station, so I decided to walk there to discuss the findings for Lou Taylor. Two days had passed since we'd found the body. The new office, built in light gray brick, looked stately from the street.

"Hey, Anna, how're you today?"

"Good. You?"

"Good. I came by to talk with Dr. Meyer."

"Yes, he's waiting for you in the examiner's office."

"Okay, thanks."

I headed down the steps and turned the corner, which led to his office and the morgue.

Dr. Meyer looked like he was on the back side of his fifties. A little worn, but in decent shape.

"How's it going?" I said.

"I'm glad it's over, that's for sure. A messy one."

"I don't want to imagine."

"You sure don't. Here's the report." He handed me a vanilla envelope with his findings. I stood there and read it. Blunt force trauma to the head caused the death. No other signs of injury or trauma on his body, except for two broken fingers on his right hand. His organs were normal except for his liver, which showed the mid-stages of liver disease.

"Do you think the fall broke his fingers?" I said.

"It's possible I guess, but not likely."

"I wouldn't think so either." I noted he'd ruled the death accidental. "The accidental ruling is fine, but I can't figure out why he would go into the woods. The only scenario I could think was him running into the woods to hide from someone or maybe he chased someone."

"Who knows the workings of a drunk mind? He may have just wandered back there." Dr. Meyer took off his glasses and cleaned them. "I want this case settled. Jan and the kids have been through enough."

"Oh, I agree. They've been put through the ringer." I said.

"Either way, it's his fault he's dead," Dr. Meyer said definitively.

"I have what I need, then. Thank you." I felt the weight of the report in my hand and questioned its validity.

CHAPTER 45

DETECTIVE WHEELER

Lush springtime grass and flowers spread over the cemetery. I stood back from the other mourners. Jessie and Brian sat by the casket alongside their mother and grandmother. I noted the kids sat by Ruth rather than their mother. She must have been the glue holding the family together. Many of Lou's fellow officers and the volunteers who helped with the search attended the funeral as well. More friends of the family than specific friends of Lou. Sadly, he didn't seem to have many friends. I guessed fellow drunks didn't attend each other's funerals.

For the tenth time, I wondered why I had come. Typically, I wouldn't attend a funeral related to a case, but the kids drew me. I wanted to watch them. The kids held the key to determining what happened to their dad.

Their movements mirrored the other. If one looked a certain direction, the other would follow suit. They sat holding hands. A girl stood behind Brian with her hands on his shoulders. Probably the girlfriend. The rest of the attendees fanned out behind them. The tall, blond boy from the search stood near the back of the mourners. He had a clear line of sight to Jessie. Another boy, with dark hair, stared at her as well, shooting hateful glances at the blond boy. Obviously, some jealousy over the girl.

Brian appeared upset, but thankfully not hysterical. I couldn't tell with Jessie. She sat still. Her primal scream the day of the search still haunted my dreams. The service concluded. As I approached, the pastor said his final farewell.

"O God, whose mercies cannot be numbered: accept our prayers on behalf of Louis Taylor and grant him an entrance into the land of light and joy, in the fellowship of thy saints; through Jesus Christ thy Son our Lord, who lives and reigns with thee and the Holy Spirit, one God, now and forever. Amen."

Jan laid a white rose on the casket. Ruth supported her, as did Brian. Jessie rose from her seat and walked away from the group toward a fountain. Her friends watched her, but hung back. I could tell they weren't sure what to do.

I wanted to talk to her. "Jessie?"

She turned around.

"I'm sorry for your loss." I said the words, but it didn't appear to be necessary.

"I'm not," she said. Her face looked older and lined, but there were no tears.

I was momentarily speechless, then said, "I'm sure you don't mean that. This must be a tough time for you."

"Whatever. Why don't you run along, detective? We don't have anything to discuss," she sneered.

"Did your dad chase you into the woods that night?" The words rolled out of my mouth.

She chuckled softly. "As I like to say, sometimes knowing is a burden. Wouldn't you agree?"

"Jessie, we're waiting for you." Brian limped over to us.

He evaluated her face. He knew. He held his hand out to her.

"Come on, let's go. Excuse us, detective." He turned away from me to lead her to the car.

"Thank you for your kind words, Detective." She winked at me.

As she walked away, I noted a long red streak down the back of her calf. It looked like someone had scratched her. My stomach dropped to the ground. What the hell just happened?

The thing I just talked to wasn't a girl. Grief didn't alter your basic personality. As much as I wanted to drop this case, I wouldn't. Brian and Jessie shared some secrets I needed to learn. As the limo pulled away, her black, soulless eyes stared back at me.

CHAPTER 46

BRIAN

Mom sobbed while Grandma tried to comfort her. I prayed they weren't paying attention to Jessie.

"Can you keep your shit together for five minutes, please?" I hissed in her ear.

"Sure, can you?" Lena said.

"Go back where you came from," I said.

"I come when she calls. She called. Deal with it. Seriously, for as much as Jessie loves you, you're a pansy. It surprises me."

"If Mom and Grandma weren't here right now, I would punch you in the face," I said.

"Your fist would never get anywhere near my face. Pansy." She sneered. "That really pisses you off. I like it. I'll remember that."

"Screw you, Lena, go back to whatever hell you came from."

"Just so you know, there is no hell. Men are so stupid. By the way, you're repeating yourself. You do realize that, I hope." She elbowed me hard in the side.

"Where's the gratitude? We're celebrating this fine day because of me. Is that what's bugging you?" She paused and stared at me with her black eyes.

"What's bugging me is you're talking too much. You're making your presence known. Jessie doesn't need that. Please, go back. I can't take this right now."

"Like I wanted to attend this shitshow," she said. "You need to understand I can't ever stay long. I wear Jessie's body out. My heart beats much faster, her body has to work a lot harder to support me."

This statement scared the shit out of me. A soulless monster inside of my sister.

"If I stayed too long, it would kill us both. Her heart, and this body can't withstand my presence," Lena said.

"Go then! Go."

She sighed and closed her eyes. "My pleasure."

Moments later her body slumped toward the door, and I felt Lena's heavy energy leave the limo. I glanced at Mom and Grandma. They hadn't noticed.

How were they oblivious to what was happening? Did they not feel her presence? It was heavy, electric. All the hair stood up on my arms whenever she took over Jessie's body. I prayed that, with Dad's passing, Lena wouldn't be needed anymore. I hoped she would disappear from our lives.

I studied Jessie's face. She was back. Lena's face appeared hard and lined. When Jessie was present those lines disappeared.

I scrubbed my face with my hands. It was too much. Dad was dead. My sister suffered from multiple personality disorder, and the big topper to this fantastic ass cake was her other personality was a psychopath. It just didn't get any better.

I leaned my head against the back of the seat and stared up at the gray ceiling of the limo. All I could do was take this one moment at a time. If I didn't, I wouldn't survive. For the first time in my life, I wanted something to make me forget or at least make me very numb. That wouldn't be an option for me, though. I would have to deal with this without the help of drugs or whatever else you could use to go numb. Thanks to dear old Dad, I knew the dangers of turning to something to make the feelings go away. I would just have to deal with it—for however long it lasted.

ABOUT THE AUTHOR

LeeAnn Werner is a marketing consul-
tant, blogger and author. LeeAnn holds a
bachelor's degree from Bowling Green State
University in Journalism. She lives in Illinois
with her wonderful husband, three beautiful
children and one super hyper dog. You can
check out her webpage and blog at www.illu-
sionofagirl.com.

Amy Goray Photography

Made in the
USA
Monee, IL